Dedalus European Classics
General Editor: Mike Mitchell

Eugene Onegin

Alexander Pushkin

Eugene Onegin

Translated with an introduction
and notes by Tom Beck

Dedalus

Published in the UK by Dedalus Ltd, Langford Lodge,
St Judith's Lane, Sawtry, Cambs, PE28 5XE
email: DedalusLimited@compuserve.com
www.dedalusbooks.com

ISBN 1 903517 28 1

Dedalus is distributed in the United States by SCB Ditsributors,
15608 South New Century Drive, Gardena, California 90248
email: info@scbdistributors.com   web site: www.scbdistributors.com

Dedalus is distributed in Australia & New Zealand by Peribo Pty Ltd,
58 Beaumont Road, Mount Kuring-gai N.S.W. 2080
email: peribo@bigpond.com

Dedalus is distributed in Canada by Marginal Distribution,
695, Westney Road South, Suite 14 Ajax, Ontario, LI6 6M9
email: marginal@marginalbook.com   web site: www.marginalbook.com

First published in Russia in 1831
First published by Dedalus in 2004

Translation, introduction and notes copyright © Tom Beck 2004

Printed in Finland by WS Bookwell
Typeset by RefineCatch, Bungay, Suffolk

THE AUTHOR

Alexander Pushkin (1799–1837) is regarded as Russia's greatest poet. From an aristocratic family he was dismissed from government service for his revolutionary epigrams. In 1832 he married Natalia Goncharova, a great beauty, but rumours of an affair with Baron Georges D'Anthès led to a duel in which Pushkin was fatally wounded. Despite his untimely death he produced a large amount of verse and narrative poetry, prose and plays of the highest quality.

THE TRANSLATOR

Tom Beck trained as a musician and has specialised in translating books about music and poetry into English from German. Inspired by a new German translation of Eugene Onegin he learnt Russian so that he could translate Eugene Onegin into English. The result is a masterpiece.

FOR MY WIFE GERALDINE

'A lily among thorns is my dearest among girls'
(*The Song of Songs* 2:2)

INTRODUCTION

Alexander Pushkin's (1799–1837) 'Novel in Verse' *Eugene Onegin* was written between the years 1823–31, and is perhaps best known outside Russia through Tchaikovsky's eponymous opera. Although the opera contains some glorious music and is deservedly popular in its own right, this popularity is nevertheless in some respects misleading, in that the opera bears as little resemblance to Pushkin's masterpiece as does many an otherwise excellent Hollywood film to the book on which it is ostensibly based. The music often verges on the sentimental, not to say mawkish, qualities about as far removed from Pushkin as can be imagined. And the libretto takes only the tragic, Hollywoodesque 'Love Story' element of the novel, which in turn is in some ways its least important aspect. Indeed, there is relatively little in Tchaikovsky's work which prepares a first-time reader of Pushkin for what the poet really intends.

There are, however, other both musical and literary parallels to Pushkin's 'Novel in Verse': on the one hand two of Mozart's most famous Italian operas, *Don Giovanni* (1787) and *Così fan tutti* (1790), and on the other Jane Austen's *Pride and Prejudice* and Byron's *Childe Harold* and *Don Juan*. Let us start with Mozart, whom Pushkin greatly admired. Don Giovanni is nominally the 'bad guy' of the opera, as is Onegin in the novel. Yet we come away from the opera feeling that of all the characters, the Don is the only one for whom we have any real sympathy. And much the same is true of Pushkin's hero Onegin, though of the ladies in the story Tatiana is a far stronger and more loveable creature than any of Don Giovanni's female victims. Both Giovanni and Onegin are willing and able not only to stand up to what life throws at them, but also to follow it through to the bitter end, something of which among all the ladies involved only Tatiana proves herself capable. Indeed, she alone among all the characters of both novel and opera is the only one who grows in stature as the story develops, while Onegin, though he sees how wrong he had been about Tatiana, remains what he always was, a dissolute rogue, as does Giovanni.

Their world is not one that we particularly admire, but given that world as a starting point, Giovanni and Onegin alone take everything in their stride that life confronts them with, while most of the other characters fall at the first hurdle. Mozart achieves this with purely musical means, allowing us, the audience, to form our own opinions of the characters. The contrast, for instance, between the two noblemen, Giovanni himself and Don Ottavio, (Donna Anna's beloved), could not be greater. Can anyone seriously imagine Ottavio taking on Giovanni? Beautiful though Ottavio's two great arias are, they also reveal him as a timid gazelle to Giovanni's hungry lion. And had he challenged the Don to a duel, his fate would doubtless have been that of Pushkin's Lenski, though Giovanni would hardly have regretted his death as Onegin immediately does.[1]

In *Così fan tutti* (a comedy of errors not dissimilar to *A Midsummer-Night's Dream*) the situation is even more extreme. The characters are all in their own way fairly abject,[2] and yet the audience leaves the spectacle wiser, reflective, and thoroughly amused, as does the reader of Pushkin's story. Mozart and Pushkin work at a number of different levels. Nominally the complex machinations of the opera are set in motion by the philosopher-sceptic Don Alfonso, as is the action of Pushkin's tale by the equally cynical Onegin. But Alfonso, in turn, is Mozart's creature (as Onegin is Pushkin's), and is thus himself given life by Mozart. Both the composer and his fictional philosopher comment on the action throughout, either directly in aria and recitative, or in purely orchestral

---

[1] Something we are made aware of after a mere few bars of the opera's opening when Giovanni quickly and ruthlessly despatches the *Commendatore*.

[2] The ladies Fiordiligi and Dorabella correspond in many ways to Olga, while Lenksi has not a few of the characteristics of Ferrando and Guglielmo.

terms. Profoundest emotions are juxtaposed in the twinkling of an eye with mock heroics and pseudo-tragedy, all carried out with a seeming ease that defies belief. The opera's action thus takes place at two removes, ostensibly set in motion by Don Alfonso but in reality by Mozart himself. And there is a third level, which constantly interweaves with the other two: the composer creating a philosopher who in turn creates the absurd comedy which creates the 'emotions-within-the emotions' we witness. We can also see Pushkin's 'Novel in Verse' in a similar way, both fictitious hero and his creator intertwined and, as it were, observing each other, while at the same time commenting on the world which the two of them inhabit, and its denizens. It is the music and the poetry which guide us through these various levels, and it is not always easy to follow quite which strand is being woven, neither in the opera nor in the poem. Indeed, so complex is the opera that until a few decades ago it was largely regarded as a failure, a lost cause, and consequently hardly performed. And even Pushkin's masterpiece took long enough to be fully recognised, not attaining the status it enjoys today until some thirty and more years after his death.

I have described those two operas at such length because more than anything else they provide us with a key with which to unlock the door to Pushkin's magic world. Far removed from the almost mundane if sometimes lush sentimentality Tchaikovsky serves up, Pushkin inhabits the scintillating world of the Mozart he so delighted in. Like the Salzburg master, he also illumines our knowledge of the world with seemingly the lightest of touches, which nevertheless reveals more than many of the world's would-be 'serious thinkers' combined. As Don Alfonso is Mozart's *alter ego* in *Così*, so is Onegin in Pushkin's novel. Neither is identical with their creator (as Pushkin is at pains to point out), yet both reflect their creators in many significant ways.

The motto of *Eugene Onegin*, apparently written in French by Pushkin himself in a letter, would seem to sum up not only the hero of Pushkin's novel, but also Don Giovanni himself, about whom Pushkin even wrote what he called a 'Little

Tragedy' in 1830, which was itself turned into an opera by Dargomizhsky (1813–69). The motto reads:

'Filled with vanity, he had even more of that kind of pride which allows a person, from a – perhaps illusory – sense of superiority, to admit to both his good and bad deeds with the same indifference.'

Yet we need not stray as far as Mozart's Italianate world to understand Pushkin's story in terms more familiar to an English-speaking readership. The main characters of Pushkin's novel are in many ways of a type already familiar to the English reader from an entirely different source, and one entirely unknown to Pushkin himself. Although the protagonists of Jane Austen's *Pride and Prejudice*, written some ten years before *Eugene Onegin* was even started, are largely those of bourgeois middle England and the minor aristocracy, whereas Pushkin's main figures belong in no small part to the high society of St. Petersburg and Moscow, there are marked similarities between the two works. Tatiana, perhaps the best-loved character in all Russian literature, is in many ways a mixture of the two oldest Bennet girls. When we first meet her she is not dissimilar to the gentle, demure and naïve Jane Bennet, trusting and quickly impressed, and also just as quickly snubbed by the man she loves. Tatiana, however, undergoes a profound change in the course of the story, and in the last chapter turns into something approaching Elizabeth Bennet as we know her at the start of Jane Austen's novel, self-assured and with a will and mind of her own. The scene in which Tatiana rejects Onegin (chapter eight) is in many ways comparable to Lizzie's rejection of Darcy when he makes his first proposal during a visit to Lady Catherine.

Onegin himself has many of the characteristics of Darcy, at least of the Darcy we meet when Jane Austen's novel begins. He, too, looks down on the simple country girls, their family, pastimes and surroundings. Indeed, in both novels it is a ballroom incident which plays a vital role in the story. Both Darcy and Onegin are so thoroughly bored by the company they find themselves in, that their future actions are dictated by what they experience. And as Darcy seeks to destroy his friend Bingley's love for Jane Bennet, so Onegin also comes between his young friend Lenski and Lenski's adored Olga, Tatiana's younger sister. Darcy, like Onegin, is at first apparently a cold and supercilious figure, whose personality develops as the story progresses. But whereas Jane Austen provides us with a happy end, Pushkin leaves his hero's fate open. Onegin comes to realise his earlier mistake, but his entreaties that the now-married and aristocratic Tatiana give him another chance are rejected, although she loves him still.[3]

Even the gallery of secondary characters in *Pride and Prejudice* is matched by Pushkin. The haughty Bingley sisters, the appalling and hysterical Mrs. Bennet (evidently a close relative of Mrs. Larin), her three foolish youngest daughters (Olga would feel at home with them, Lydia in particular), the sycophantic Mr. Collins and his snobbish patroness Lady Catherine all find their parallels in Pushkin's novel, which can perhaps best be approached by an English-speaking reader as a Russian counterpart to Jane Austen's masterpiece.

There is, however, one obvious difference between the two works. While Jane Austen writes the most delectable prose, Pushkin's is a tale told in equally delightful verse. His model for a story in verse was Byron, and in particular *Childe Harold's Pilgrimage* (1812–18) and *Don Juan* (1819–24). Pushkin read Byron in French translations, which were enormously popular, if not very good. Nabokov tells us that Pushkin attempted to learn English, but with little success, and even thought the word 'Childe' was pronounced 'chilled'! His initial attitude to Byron was enthusiastic, but this cooled to respect, rather than affection. There are various references to the English poet in *Eugene Onegin*, and all of them reflect Pushkin's growing sense of distance to his erstwhile model. Many of the devices we find in *Onegin* would appear to have their origins in *Don Juan*.

---

[3] Even here there is an echo of Mozart, the closing scene of *Le nozze di Figaro* (1786), though the forgiveness granted Figaro and the Count does not extend to Onegin.

Both poets play with the difficulty of translating from one language (French) into their own, both employ lists of names to score some mocking point or other, both heroes have their difficulties with Latin and the classics in general, though the authors themselves refer to various writers of the ancient world with whom they themselves are perfectly familiar. The childhood days of Juan and Eugene, and their upbringing, are decidedly similar. Both are dissatisfied with life as they find it as young men, and the value of a legacy from the unexpected death of some aged relative is ironically stressed. One could go on. Digressions from the main theme, conversations within the structure of the verse, witty endings to a verse or chapter, deflating irony, the mocking of some fellow poets, the admiration for others, even descriptions of rooms which the respective heroes inhabit, they are all to be found in Byron and Pushkin.

The differences, however, are much greater. The idea of using sonnets for the novel was entirely Pushkin's own. Writing came easily to both poets, but while Byron's pen all too often seems to run away with him, leading to a verbosity which can at times try the patience of even the most devoted, Pushkin is a master of concentrated structure. As with the Mozart he so admired, everything is essential and thus infinitely more effective. Both Pushkin and Mozart can modulate from major to minor and back again, from gaiety to tragedy, from despair to laughter, from deepest insight into human nature to the ironic observation of their fellow men, effortlessly and in an instant. Poet and musician play with their respective art forms with a virtuosity that is uniquely breathtaking, and both produce music of the highest quality and the greatest beauty, unmatched in its own particular way either before or since.

The story of Eugene Onegin is one of realistic, turbulent, and ultimately unfulfilled love, which in some respects looks forward to the twentieth century. Pushkin does not allow the fractured circle of emotions to be closed by a classic nineteenth century happy-end. Onegin, a handsome stranger, having been left a legacy, appears one day from fashionable

St. Petersburg in the provincial place where Tatiana lives. Though quickly disenchanted with country life, he is brought together with and befriends a young man and naïve poet, Lenski, who has arrived from Germany. Lenski falls in love with Tatiana's younger sister, Olga, to whom he soon becomes engaged. Much as Bingley does with Darcy, Lenski drags the bored Onegin to meet his Olga, where Tatiana sees and is profoundly attracted to him. Having written him a letter declaring her love, she is coldly rejected. Once more Onegin is taken to the Larins' house for Tatiana's name day, where (as with Darcy) the rural celebrations infuriate him. Annoyed that his friend Lenski should have exposed him to such an imposition, he flirts outrageously with Olga. Lenski challenges him to a duel, is killed, and Olga promptly marries someone else.

Tatiana, still unwed, is taken to Moscow to find a husband and married off to a prince and general in the Russian army. Returning to St. Petersburg from his travels, undertaken in an attempt to forget the killing of his young friend, Onegin sees Tatiana at a ball, and this time he becomes obsessed by her. In his turn, he, too, writes a letter declaring his passion for her, is rejected, though Tatiana does admit that she still loves him and . . . Then what? We never find out, for Pushkin breaks off his tale at this point and rounds his novel off with a few reflective and valedictory verses. We do not even have the fascination of discovering, as we do in *Pride and Prejudice*, how or even whether this unlikely pair finally get together.

Apart from the two lengthy letters which Tatiana and Onegin respectively write to each other (of which Tatiana's is regarded as one of the great moments of Russian literature, perhaps not unlike Hamlet's 'To be, or not to be . . .' monologue for the reader of English), there are three further noteworthy episodes. These are Tatiana's dream in chapter five, the duel between Onegin and Lenski in chapter six, and Tatiana's visit to Onegin's house in chapter seven (once he has gone on his travels), when she for the first time realises his true and apparently shallow nature. At this point there is a contrast with Lizzie Bennet's visit to Pemberley, when she for the first time recognises that Darcy is in fact the very opposite of what she had imagined. The dream sequence foreshadows, in a mixture of comic adventures and grotesque images, the events leading to Lenski's death, while mirroring Tatiana's confused state of mind concerning Onegin. The duel scene contains some of the finest imagery in the entire poem, as Lenski's death is described. And to the reader who remembers that Pushkin himself died in just such circumstances a few years after the completion of his masterpiece, this episode takes on an almost unbearable poignancy. Finally there are Tatiana's visits to Onegin's house, which reveal her as a shy, sensitive and naïve country girl, who in the most unexpected fashion is brought to see the truth about the man she has loved, which we, the readers, already know from chapter one in particular.

This brief account of the narrative throws light on one of its main characteristics: Pushkin's preoccupation with real people and real things. *Eugene Onegin* is filled with the most striking portraits of people from all walks of life, both in the city and the country. The social life of St. Petersburg and Moscow, the theatres, the great receptions and balls, street scenes from both these cities on the one hand, and the simpler rustic jollifications, the rural inhabitants of Tatiana's provincial home and surroundings on the other, are all presented with complete authenticity. Certainly, as with Jane Austen, there is often an element of parody or even downright malice in the portrayals, but that merely adds to the sense of realism, as we see Pushkin probing below the surface, not content with merely delineating outer appearances. Even Nature itself can be both beautiful, as in the many sonnets echoing its delights, or, as in Tatiana's dream, terrifying. And neither is the animal world excluded: a shaggy bear, initially frightening and finally kindly, accompanies Tatiana in her dream, while the goose trying to go for a swim in an ice-covered river in chapter four has become legendary in Russian literature. Pushkin's is not a romantic world, but a realistic one, in which things are as they are. Boris Pasternak, in his great novel about a poet, *Dr. Zhivago*, has his hero write in a diary entry about Pushkin:

'It's as if the air, the light, the noise of life, of real substantial things burst into his poetry from the street as through an open window. Concrete things – things in the outside world, things in current use, names of things, common nouns – crowd in and take possession of his verse, driving out the vaguer parts of speech. Things and more things, lined up in rhymed columns on the page.'[4]

It is Pushkin's eye for detail, his delight in what he sees that removes from even the tragic scenes of the novel any trace of mawkishness or cloying sentimentality. Pushkin loves humanity with all its virtues and failings, and so he does not attempt to idealise the world or the people who live in it. There is no 'Good' or 'Bad', just life as we all experience it, a mixture of both which deserves neither condemnation nor praise, because it is what it is: our world. We do not transcend the world, but are reconciled to it, and enjoy what it has to give, without trying to flee into some paradise beyond. Music, theatre, poetry, whether accomplished or not, tragedy and joy, a little wisdom and absurdity in abundance, artistry and sexuality, they are all there, and Pushkin, and we with him, are glad of it. We do not crave more than is on offer, but realise that such is our world and we learn to accept and love that world for its own sake. It is not a coherent 'philosophy' with which the poet presents us, it is more: it is us as we are, 'warts and all'. The leading British Pushkin scholar A. D. P. Briggs quotes S. L. Frank in *Alexander Pushkin, a critical study*:[5]

'Aldous Huxley . . . has rightly observed that although Mozart's music seems gay, it is in fact sad. The same can be said about the poetry of Pushkin . . . the explanation is the same in both cases. The artistic expression of sorrow, grief and the tragic is so filled with the light from some quiet, unearthly, angelic sense of

---

[4] Translated M. Haywood and M. Harari (Collins and Harvill Press, London, 1958, pp. 257–8).
[5] The Bristol Press, 1991, p. 211

reconciliation and enlightenment that the content appears joyful.'

Much has been written on the relationship between Pushkin himself and his hero. Although the poet distinguishes at all times between himself, Onegin, and Byron, it is not difficult to see similarities between the dissolute fictional dandy from St. Petersburg and Pushkin himself, whose dissipation, even by the standards of his own time, was remarkable. Both were also womanisers, and both fought duels over women: Onegin as the result of his own foolishness, killing his friend, while Pushkin himself was killed in a duel following rumours that his wife was having an affair with the Baron Georges d'Anthès, the adopted son of the Dutch Ambassador. The whole extraordinary story is brilliantly and excitingly told by Serena Vitale.[6] Pushkin constantly imposes himself on the story, either with comments on the characters he is describing, or with comments about himself, his past life, society in general, his feelings about nature and the countryside, city life, his longing for Italy or even Africa, whence his great grandfather had come and of whom he was inordinately proud. At one point he even describes a meeting with his hero and their mutual admiration. And yet Onegin is in many ways pure fiction, if ultimately derived from Byron's melancholy and defiant outcast *Childe Harold* on the one hand, and the delightfully witty *Don Juan* on the other. Three times Onegin is explicitly compared to Childe Harold, while Tatiana, visiting Onegin's deserted house wonders whether he might not even be 'a Muscovite in Harold's cloak.'

Onegin is thus a kind of 'pick-and-mix', containing both elements of Pushkin himself, and Byron's two most famous poetic heroes, *Childe Harold* and *Don Juan*, themselves based on Byron's own life and experiences. Pushkin's attitude towards his hero in many ways resembles his feelings about the English poet he once so admired, but now felt increasingly distant from, as he makes clear in a number of passages in

[6] *Pushkin's Button*, London 1999

Eugene Onegin itself. Indeed, it is tempting to see the relationship between the two poets mirrored in that of Tatiana and Onegin themselves. Initially Tatiana is completely enamoured of Onegin, as was Pushkin of Byron, while at the end of the novel, though still loving him, she rejects him for her new life and position in society. Tatiana, the most purely human of all the characters in the novel, the one in whom Pushkin invested the tender side of his own personality, can thus be seen as the embodiment of the love the poet felt for his English forebear, who is finally cast off to be replaced by Russian life, language and literature.

Formal Considerations

The Pushkin sonnet uses an extremely flexible iambic tetrameter,[7] which lends the stanzas a fairly fast pace (*andante con moto*). The scheme on which each is built is as follows, illustrated by the first sonnet of chapter one. The letters and numbers at the end of each line represent the end-rhymes, while the subscript numbers indicate the feet per line, 9 indicating a weak and 8 a strong ending:

"My uncle's acted very wisely,	A_9
to seek his bed when he's so sick;	B_8
his family's reacted nicely	A_9
and he's most happy with his trick.	B_8
He's set the world a good example,	C_9
which others would do well to sample,	C_9
but it's a bore, when night and day	D_8
the sick man forces you to stay!	D_8
To keep him sweet, as if he's dying,	E_9
give him his daily medicine	F_8
and make quite sure that it goes in,	F_8
adjust the pillows while one's sighing:	E_9

---

[7] A weakly stressed syllable followed by a strong one, of which there are four in each line.

> 'Don't even *think* of getting well, G_8
> the devil take you, go to hell!' " G_8

The *Eugene Onegin* sonnet divides up into three sections: lines 1–4, 5–12, 13–14. The first four lines present the essential subject of the stanza, the following eight allow a discourse on it, while the final two serve either as a kind of summary in the more serious passages, or bring it to a spirited conclusion in the more light-hearted verses. It is thus a highly flexible construction, which is, however, never allowed to dictate the actual nature of the writing, the sentence structure and the like. Pushkin also makes frequent use of enjambment,[8] and even on occasion to great effect between two separate sonnets, connecting them to each other, thus extending the freedoms available to him. From a purely professional point of view, the first four lines are the most difficult to render into English. They set the tone of what follows, and have to 'work' within the strict confines of the quatrain. The next eight lines allow one to spread one's wings, while the final couplet gives the writer a chance to be 'clever', show what one can do, a little like a *cadenza* in a concerto.

The differences between Russian and English make countless compromises necessary. The order of certain lines has to be altered, words have to be changed (an impatient horse might snort or shake its head in Pushkin, but stamp in my version, if it suits the needs of rhyme and rhythm). Many Russian words are longer than their English equivalents, which means that certain adjustments are inevitable. Furthermore, Russian sentence structure is different, which means that certain elements of the original have to be sacrificed. Some sonnets of the original, for instance, are made up of one single sentence. In the interests of lucidity this has at times had to be abandoned, as the greater number of words required in English can lead to confusion of meaning, if the same trick is attempted in the translation. Sonnet 20 of chapter eight is a

---

[8] A phrase or sentence which does not end with the line, but carries on to the next one(s).

case in point: the original is made up of 59 words in a single sentence, a question, while my version contains 94 words, and three separate question marks.

A Note on the Translation

Having been brought up initially speaking Czech, and later English and German, as a passionate admirer of Stravinsky, I eventually developed a reading knowledge of Russian, though my research in the 1960s with Egon Wellesz at Oxford centred on Viennese 12-tone music, art and thought. English and German remained my two native languages, and I later wrote for both English and German publications, also translating poetry and plays from German into English and vice versa. I had known *Eugene Onegin* for some considerable time, but the idea of actually translating it into English only came to me decades later purely by chance. My wife, returning from a visit to friends in Germany, brought with her three cassettes on which the great actor Gerd Westphal read Ulrich Busch's German version of the poem.[9] This had proved immensely popular in German-speaking countries, and were it not a 'mere' translation, it would surely be required reading for every student of the German language.

In 1964 Vladimir Nabokov had published his famous and notoriously eccentric English rendering of the work, literal, composed in shadowy iambics, completely without rhyme, and at times almost incomprehensible. So great was his love for Pushkin's masterpiece, that he felt to attempt any more would be a desecration of the work. In spite of its manifold oddities, the translation and the magnificent 1000 page commentary Nabokov produced, remain essential reading for anyone who wishes to delve deeper into *Eugene Onegin*. What Busch, however, showed was that it is possible to produce a translation which is a true work of art in its own right. Using, as I have also done, not only normal rhyme, but also

[9] Manesse Verlag, Zurich, 1981.

occasionally devices such as half-rhyme and assonance,[10] and permitting himself a certain degree of freedom, enabled Busch to cope with perhaps the greatest problem facing a translator: making the result sound as if it actually might have been written in the language into which it has been transported. And if such a feat could be accomplished in German, then why not in English? This translation is an attempt to answer that question.

For various reasons (censorship, or fear of it, being perhaps the main one) Pushkin left out a number of sonnets, and even individual lines. The omitted sonnets have been indicated by the number they would have had, while other missing passages are indicated by a broken line.

[10] Vowel rhyme

ACKNOWLEDGEMENTS

It is my pleasant duty to proffer my profoundest thanks to two people in particular, whose help in this project has been of inestimable value. First I must thank my wife, who first introduced me to Ulrich Busch's German version. She has read and re-read every word of the English text, made countless enormously valuable suggestions, proof-read and checked the manuscript time and again, and remained cheerfully encouraging those many times when I could no longer contemplate finishing another sonnet, let alone completing the whole novel. Then there is my editor, Mike Mitchell of Dedalus, who has likewise read every word through many times. He displayed both patience and humour in his dealings with me, his comments and many suggestions were always eminently intelligent and perceptive, while his refusal simply to allow me my own way prompted a huge variety of ideas and improvements. Mike in some ways had the easier task, for he had to bear my doubts and occasional spells of impatience from the other end of an e-mail connection. My wife was heroically obliged to put up with me at first hand, never an easy task at the best of times . . . I have also received some most useful help from the staff at Dedalus Books. All have contributed immeasurably to whatever merits this translation might have. Its failings, needless to say, are entirely my own work.

I have already mentioned the curious literal translation and extraordinarily brilliant commentary by Vladimir Nabokov, which were invaluable to me, as to everyone else who has delved further into this work, and which I can only recommend to all those whose interest might have been aroused by the present version of *Eugene Onegin*. Ulrich Busch's superb German version ignited the spark of insight as to how the task of making an enjoyable English version of *Eugene Onegin* might be undertaken. Also consulted were A. D. P. Briggs' useful study of Pushkin, Elaine Feinstein's monograph on the poet, and T. J. Binyon's monumental and splendid biography.

EUGENE ONEGIN

A Novel in Verse
Alexander Pushkin

Pétri de vanité il avait encore plus de cette espèce
d'orgueil qui fait avouer avec la même indifférence les
bonnes comme les mauvaises actions, suite d'un sentiment
de supériorité, peut-être imaginaire.

Tiré d'une lettre particulière

TO PETER ALEXANDROVICH PLETNEV

Not thinking just of entertaining
society, but dear friends too,
I wish my gift were more sustaining
and worthier of all of you,
more worthy of a noble spirit,
replete with an immortal dream,
with poetry so clear and vivid
which simply and sublimely gleams,
brimful of lofty thoughts. So be it.
Now take this work of motley tales,
half humorous, half melancholy,
humanely told, and popularly,
the careless fruits of fun and pale
insomniac imagination,
neglectful, sterile withered years,
the intellect's cold observation
and then the heart's unhappy fears.

CHAPTER ONE

To live it hurries and to feel it hastes . . .
Prince Vyazemski

CHAPTER ONE

1

"My uncle's acted very wisely,
to seek his bed when he's so sick;
his family's reacted nicely
and he's most happy with his trick.
He's set the world a good example,
which others really ought to sample,
but it's a bore, when night and day
the sick man forces you to stay!
To keep him sweet, as if he's dying,
give him his daily medicine
and make quite sure that it goes in,
adjust the pillows while one's sighing:
'Don't even *think* of getting well,
the devil take you, go to hell!' "

2

Thus thought a ne'er–do–well and dandy
whom Zeus had made his uncle's heir:
to him the money'd come in handy,
so coach and horses rushed him there.
For those who love my comic thriller
of Ruslan and his dear Ludmilla,
I'll introduce without ado,
the hero of my tale to you:
Onegin, whom I've long befriended,
had grown up on the Neva's shore,
perhaps like you, dear reader, for
St. Petersburg is truly splendid
where once we wandered back and forth,
though now I really hate the North.

3

Completing service long and faithful,
his father ended his career
and left his son debts by the plateful
from having given balls each year.
And yet my friend was saved from Hades
by his Madame, a Gallic lady;
and then Monsieur took on the lad,
a lively child but never bad.
Monsieur l'abbé, who hated quarrels,
thought learning ought to be a joy,
tried not to overwhelm the boy.
He didn't bother him with morals,
and if annoyed, he didn't bark,
but took Eugene to Letny Park.

4

When Eugene grew and first felt passion,
was plagued by love and hope and doubt,
they did what's always been the fashion
and threw the wretched abbé out.
My friend was free from every pressure,
could live and act as was his pleasure,
so he was always finely dressed
in what was surely London's best.
He spoke and wrote French to perfection,
bowed constantly, his hair well curled,
and when he danced he turned and twirled,
his light Mazurka no exception.
He didn't have too long to wait
before the world thought he was great.

5

We all of us have had some schooling,
a bit of this, a bit of that,
and so not too much art in fooling
the world is needed when we chat.
Eugene was thought by everybody
(assessors neither soft nor shoddy)
a learned if pedantic man,
and one of those who always can
well hold his own in conversation,
who easily can prate and talk
of anything, but never balk
at listening with concentration,
whose epigrams once in a while
would make the ladies blush and smile.

6

Though people have stopped learning Latin,
he nonetheless could always quote
some Juvenal, three verses that in
his lessons he had learned by rote,
could talk about the Roman poets
and sign his letters, would you know it,
with *vale*, knew imperfectly
two lines of Virgil and, though he
had very little inclination
to bother with the distant past,
with what came first and what came last,
told anecdotes with dedication
which started with Rome's Romulus
and stretched through time right down to us.

7

He couldn't see why poets suffer
or live and struggle for their art,
nor could he keep, though not a duffer,
iambics and trochees apart.
Theocritus and even Homer
induced in him a kind of coma,
but well informed on Adam Smith,
he knew what made men poor or rich.
He understood the wealth of nations,
what happens when a product's sold
and how to manage without gold,
explained all this with utmost patience.
His father failed to understand
and quickly mortgaged all his land.

8

There'd be but little point in trying
to catalogue what Eugene knew,
and yet there can be no denying,
for it's unquestionably true,
that he devoted all his talents
to vain attempts to curb and balance
the anguish, torments, toil and joy
of lifelong passion since a boy:
the tender art of ardent yearning
of which the poet Ovid wrote
and then was banished to remote
Moldavian steppes in which the burning
desires declined and from whence he
could not return to Italy.

9/10

Eugene soon learned how to dissemble,
to hide his hopes, show jealousy,
to pine away, or shyly tremble,
comport himself obediently,
to be indifferent or attentive,
and make his letters so inventive,
now casual, now eloquent
or passionate when he unbent.
By turns he could be cold or charming,
aloof or loving in his ways,
put charm or scorn into his gaze,
which one and all found quite disarming
in such a man of youthful years
who never tried to hide his tears.

11

He varied his appearance daily,
admired anew by one and all,
could frown, deceive and just as gaily
crack jokes and flatter in a drawl,
or suddenly be touching, tender,
wake passion in the gentler gender,
could longingly both sigh and plead,
encourage and then urge his need,
demand a loving, coy confession
while listening to a beating heart,
of which he'd made a subtle art:
that always made a deep impression.
He knew then what he had to do
and taught the girls a thing or two!

12

He quickly learned to make hearts flutter
in even fast and loose coquettes,
would often make his rivals splutter
with rage, while he had no regrets.
He'd sometimes spread a nasty rumour,
his rivals' anger fuelled his humour;
to married men he was a friend,
someone on whom they could depend.
Ignoring all, they curried favour –
as worthy students of Faublas –
they shunned the threat of an éclat,
and put up with his strange behaviour;
each husband sat down with his wife
at table, satisfied with life.

13, 14, 15

At times as he was blithely dreaming,
(he loved to have a nap, or sprawl),
a note arrived for him *"esteeming
his presence"* at that evening's ball,
"For lunch" or *"at the children's party,"*
the greeting always warm and hearty.
Where should my scapegrace go from here?
Where should he start? He's no idea.
But never mind, it's not important.
He drives along the boulevard
parading his broad bolivar,
or strolls around with proud deportment,
until the sounds of Bréguet's chime
remind him that it's time to dine.

16

The evening's come, it's dark already,
as Eugene climbs into his sleigh,
his collar wet from snowy eddies.
The driver shouts "Make way, make way!"
At Talon's friend Kavérin's waiting
for them to start their celebrating;
the wine's already standing there,
and merriment is in the air.
Some roast beef's piled upon a platter
and truffles, youthful luxury,
the best of Gallic cookery
with Limburg cheese and jolly chatter,
and pineapple, Strasbourg pâté
round off a simply marvellous day.

17

They keep on calling out for glasses
of wine to cool off the flambé,
forget how rapidly time passes –
Eugene is due at the ballet,
where he will play the knowing critic,
at times benign, at times acerbic,
a devotee of show and stage,
who's always ready to engage
in hissing at the scheming Phaedra,
applaud a brilliant *entrechat*,
divine in rippling taffeta,
acclaim Moena, Cleopatra,
or – just in order to be heard –
to give the spectacle the bird!

18

A magic world in which Fonvízin
lampooned mankind quite without fear,
Knyazhnín revamped what was in season,
while Ózerov would jerk a tear
with plays in which young Sémyonóva
enchanted every Casanova;
Katénin showed us how to play
the genius of the great Corneille,
where Sháhovskóy, unruly, caustic,
received the plaudits of the crowd
for comedies both fast and loud,
and Didelot's ballets, majestic
décor and dancing shone and gleamed
was where I spent my youth, and dreamed.

19

My goddesses! Where have you vanished?
Can you still hear my mournful voice,
or have you all been long since banished?
Do others now provide the joys,
(although they cannot take your places),
you dear terpsichorean graces,
so soulful once, so full of light,
who were my evening's great delight?
Or will my doleful gaze, now weary
of alien stages, my lorgnette
alight on gaiety which yet
leaves me indifferent, feeling dreary,
as I remember with a sigh
the happiness of years gone by?

20

The house is full, the boxes shining,
the audience impatiently
is seething. Now the curtain's rising,
there's clapping in the gallery!
Ethereal and quite resplendent
a throng of nymph and elf attendants,
to violins' alluring sound,
advance and daintily surround
Istómina, who's slowly spinning,
as light as air, a piece of fluff
that floats upon a zephyr's puff,
a ballerina, graceful, winning;
her twirling feet appear to fly
and lissom leaps enchant the eye.

21

Applause rings out. Onegin enters.
He treads upon the people's toes
and looks about, his lorgnette centres
upon the ladies whom he knows.
He scans the tiers, a sea of faces,
salutes the men, goes through his paces.
Observing how the girls are dressed,
he certainly is not impressed;
while lost in sober contemplation
he glances round him with a yawn
and what he sees fills him with scorn.
He thinks with mounting indignation
that he has really had enough
of Didelot's insipid stuff.

22

The stage is full of cupids, serpents
and dancing devils, such-like folk,
while in the porch the tired servants
are sleeping on their master's cloak.
The audience is busy coughing
or clapping, laughing, loudly scoffing,
and outside, inside, everywhere
bright lanterns light the winter air.
The horses fidget, bored and freezing,
the coachmen warm their hands and wait,
they curse their masters, it's so late,
and soon they too are also sneezing.
But our Onegin's long since gone,
he's got some new clothes to try on.

23

May I describe, with your permission,
Eugene's secluded dressing-room
in which that devotee of fashion
would dress, undress, spray on perfume?
The novelties London produces
are sent to Russia to seduce us,
all in exchange for wax and wood
which we export for tawdry goods.
Whatever comes from modish Paris,
the fripperies for every taste
and those with cash enough to waste,
creations of Parisian prowess,
they all were purchased by our sage,
so wise at eighteen years of age.

24

There lies a pipe of finest amber,
an artefact of Istanbul,
aromas which he used to pamper
himself, intense and plentiful,
some files and combs, assorted scissors,
and thirty brushes, diverse clippers,
fine bronzes and rich porcelain,
the very best he could obtain.
Rousseau (forgive me the digression)
could never understand how Grimm
dared clean his nails in front of *him*,
the crackpot with his odd obsessions;
our advocate of liberty
was wrong, and that entirely!

25

A man can be indeed efficient
and yet ensure his nails are clean;
it's you, not fashion that's deficient,
for custom's always ruled the scene!
Afraid of jealous condescension,
Onegin paid supreme attention
to how he looked, and how he dressed.
A fop, he only wore the best,
he'd spend three hours at his mirror
assuaging his sartorial urge
till he was ready to emerge
appearing every inch a winner,
a manly Venus on parade
while mincing to a masquerade.

26

From head to foot he was attired
in clothes of greatest elegance,
which those around him much admired
and would engage *your* curious glance.
How I would love to paint his picture
and not arouse your angry stricture;
a writer's job is to describe,
I can already hear you gibe.
My style's too poor, I must admit it,
for "pantaloons", "waistcoat" and "frock",
they are not words of Russian stock,
and so in every way unfitted
for verse: I've had a look to see
and they're not in the dictionary.

27

But that's not our concern at present,
we'd better hurry to the ball:
Onegin's gone to have a pleasant
soirée before the curtains fall.
We pass a row of slumbering houses,
along a street which gently drowses,
the gleaming lamps of smart coupés
all travelling their different ways,
some passing by a splendid villa,
projecting rainbows on the snow
which seem to make it warmly glow.
Behind the lighted windows glimmer
bejewelled ladies showing off
and shadows of a foppish toff.

28

Our hero has now reached the entrance
and, rushing up the palace stair,
impatient almost past endurance,
he runs his fingers through his hair.
The ballroom's full of dancers swaying,
by now the band is sick of playing,
mazurkas make the dancers flush
and almost faint beneath the crush.
We hear the sound of spurs that jingle
as officers and ladies dance,
each casts a captivating glance
at socialites who blithely mingle:
their jealous whispering is drowned
by clamouring orchestral sound.

29

In days of gaiety and longing
I loved to go to every ball,
where passing notes amidst the thronging
array's not difficult at all,
while vowing love is oh so easy
among the dancers, bright and breezy . . .
Respected husbands, please beware,
and all you mothers take good care
to mark my words or you'll be sorry.
Observe your daughters, never let
them out of range of your lorgnette
or else . . . may God spare you the worry!
I'll lay the law down hard and fast
because *my* sins lie in the past!

30

I have, alas, had lots of pleasure,
have often squandered day and night,
and had my morals in some measure
not suffered, I would still delight
in balls with all their frenzied madness,
the crush, the glitter and the gladness
of girls and ladies choicely dressed,
I love their little feet the best.
In all of Russia you will never
locate three pairs of ladies' feet
which are both feminine and neat,
but I'll remember two for ever,
two little feet . . . they haunt my thoughts
at night when I am overwrought.

31

Oh little feet, where are you strolling?
I'm such a fool, let me forget!
Oh little feet, are you extolling
the verdant springtime flowers yet?
Brought up in oriental warmness,
you loved the luxury of flawless
and yielding rugs beneath your toes,
which left no marks on northern snows.
Have I forgotten my obsession,
my longing for a poet's fame,
abandoned hope to make my name
for you, borne exile and oppression?
The happiness of youth, alas!
has passed like footsteps on the grass.

32

Ah, Flora's cheeks, Diana's bosom
are fetching, as you know, my friends!
Terpsichore's small feet are winsome,
yes, they're the ones I most commend,
for they are full of priceless promise,
of pleasure, charm, and luscious longings.
Those are the feet which I adore
and think of daily more and more:
beneath the tablecloth's soft billows,
(cloth made of damask, edged with lace),
in winter by the fireplace,
in springtime leas, by greening willows,
at brilliant, incandescent balls,
near thunderous waves on sea-girt walls.

33

When I recall the tempests blowing
I envy each and every wave
that's lovingly and wildly flowing
towards those feet I also crave.
Oh how I longed to join those waters
and kiss those feet, so dear and faultless!
No, never in those fiery days
when I indulged in youthful ways,
did I experience such a torment,
desire to kiss Armidas' lips,
their pining breasts, their rounded hips,
those ruby cheeks, so soft and fervent,
No, never did such great distress
afflict me then, I must confess!

34

And there are times when I remember
with trepidation now and then,
a foot, a stirrup, cherished, tender,
which I once held . . . both where and when . . .
Again in my imagination
I touch that foot in fascination;
the blood is surging in my heart,
now wizened, wasted as it smarts . . .
But that's enough! I've sung their praises
too much upon my babbling lyre,
yet they're not worth what they inspire,
my verses for those haughty ladies,
whose words and gazes speak deceit
as much as do their little feet.

35

And my Onegin? He's now yawning
as he drives home from ball to bed.
St. Petersburg is roused, it's morning,
a drum tells all that night has fled.
The merchant's up, the vendor's hawking,
the cabman's coming, slowly walking,
the milk-girl hurries on her way
on crunching snow at break of day.
The sounds of sunrise have now started,
the shutters open, chimney smoke
is rising as the fires are stoked.
The German baker has departed
in cotton cap, punctiliously,
to open up his bakery.

36

Exhausted by the noisy evening,
transforming daytime into night,
he's blissfully asleep and dreaming,
a child of revels and delight.
It will be midday when he rises,
but there will be no great surprises,
his life will go on as before,
monotonous and motley, more
of much the same routine enchantment.
But was my Eugene satisfied?
He took his conquests in his stride,
was young and free, and always ardent.
Yet was he happy living thus,
amid the banquets and the fuss?

37

Alas! His feelings were now cooling,
he wearied of the social round,
the constant flirting and the fooling
now seemed to him absurd, unsound.
Pursuing beauties now fatigued him,
betrayals, friends no more intrigued him,
nor guzzling beefsteaks, Strasbourg Pie,
champagne until the day you die,
dispensing piquant sayings, grimace,
and bicker, have an aching head
from everything you've done and said.
Although he was a fiery scapegrace,
he'd lost his love of having fun,
of sabre-fighting and the gun.

38

He was not well! Occasionally
it was quite like the English "spleen",
in short, a Russian "melancholy",
the cause of which should long have been
found out! It overcame him slowly
and left him feeling languid, lowly.
To shoot himself seemed quite unfair
and thank the Lord, he didn't dare!
Childe Harold-like, he was ill-humoured,
stopped gossiping and playing cards,
was cold and distant, almost hard,
a glance, a sigh, it soon was rumoured,
no longer fascinated him:
he soon became so dull and prim.

39, 40, 41
42

It was the flighty and capricious
attractive ladies he ignored;
the upper class is meretricious
and he was very quickly bored.
Although he now and then had heard them
interpret works by Say or Bentham,
their conversation mostly was
but little more than harmless tosh.
The ladies were both pure and stainless,
so stately, so intelligent,
so piously extravagant,
so thoughtful they were simply blameless,
unreachable and so serene,
they gave the men the English spleen!

43

And you, my lovely, gorgeous cuties
whom droshkies carry every night
across St. Petersburg, my beauties,
he's left you high and dry alright!
For my Eugene there's no enjoyment,
he's found himself a new employment:
now shut away within his room,
he took a pen and, filled with gloom,
began to write, but soon was yawning,
for too much effort made him ill,
and not a word spilled from his quill.
So don't assume he'll be adorning
the list of those I'll not condemn,
for I am also one of them.

44

And in his self-imposed detention,
oppressed by sloth, and quite alone,
he settled down with the intention
of making others' thoughts his own.
His books paraded just like soldiers
but nothing came from all his boldness;
however much he skimmed and read
nothing at all stuck in his head.
This tome was dull and that too sober,
he found the old books stiff and cold,
the new ones raged against the old.
He'd left the girls, ceased poring over
his barren books, but let them stand,
an army lamed and quite unmanned.

45

I, too, had cast the world's conventions
aside, abandoned vain pursuits.
I met him then, and let me mention
how much I prized his attributes,
his love of musing and of dreaming,
his oddities, so curious seeming,
a razor-sharp and biting mind,
for I was bitter, he unkind.
Familiar with the play of passion,
in us the fires no longer glowed,
we both were bowed beneath the load
of fate, both victims of oppression,
of blind Fortuna and of men:
our lives were just beginning then.

46

A living and a thinking being
despises people in all ways,
a feeling man must find disturbing
the ghosts of dead and buried days;
for him there's now no more enjoyment,
our memories are like a serpent
and like repentance, they will bite.
All this, of course, can lend delight
and zest to any conversation.
Initially I was bemused,
his tartness shocked, but soon grew used
to all his banter, condemnation,
the wit combined with acid bile,
the gloomy epigrams and guile.

47

How often when the sky's transparent
in summer, when the night's aglow,
Diana's face is not apparent
down in the river's depths below;
at times like these we'd both remember
intrigues, past loves, both bitter, tender,
responsive, carefree once again,
we drank the evening's breath in then,
benign and silent, like some convict
moved dazed and sleepy from his cell
to forest glades and forest smells,
transported by a magic edict,
so we'd be borne off by a dream
to some new life, so it would seem.

48

Eugene was filled with pensive sadness
while he was standing by the shore,
regrets suffused his thoughtful soul, as
the poet sang some years before.
The night was still, the calls of sentries
resounded, with the noise of droshkies
clip-clopping in the distance from
the Mil'onnaya with aplomb.
A lonely boat was slowly skimming
along the dozing riverside,
a horn then echoed far and wide,
a captivating voice was singing,
yet sweeter than the sounds we heard
are those of Tasso's magic words.

49

Oh waves of Adria, of Brenta,
your waters, too, have made me dream
of seeing you, that I may enter
your world of inspiration, seem
to hear your magic voice and follow
that river, sacred to Apollo's
descendants, also known to me
from Albion's lyre across the sea.
I'll there enjoy the sensuous freedom
of golden nights in Italy,
Venetian beauty next to me,
first mute, then fulsome, charming, buxom,
and kissing in a gondola,
I'll find the tongue of Petrarca.

50

When will the hour of freedom beckon?
The time has come, let it not fail;
I roam the heights and hope that heaven
permits a boat to show its sail.
Oh when beneath the raging thunder,
which cloaks the ocean as I wander,
shall I start out upon the course
which frees me from these dreary shores?
To me they've now become so painful
though I, across the seas afar
beneath the skies of Africa,
would sigh for Russia, sombre, baleful,
where once I loved, was once distressed,
and where I laid my heart to rest.

51

Onegin was prepared to travel
and visit alien lands with me,
but all our plans would soon unravel
as fate's hand intervened and we
were parted when Onegin's pater
went suddenly to meet his maker.
His creditors all swarmed about,
but Eugene quickly threw them out.
He hated any litigation
and, quite contented with his lot,
relinquished all that he had got,
perceived no cause for agitation.
Perhaps the thought was in his head
that soon his uncle would be dead.

52

A missive came all of a sudden
in which Eugene was notified
of his declining uncle's summons
to take his leave before he died.
When he had read this tragic letter,
he started out, now feeling better,
with but one single aim in view
he rushed off to the rendezvous.
Though yawning in anticipation,
he was prepared, for money's sake,
to cheat, be bored, to stay awake
(with which I started my narration).
When he arrived he only found
a tribute ready for the ground.

53

The house, he saw, was full of mourners,
as former foes and former pals
showed up to grieve from all four corners,
all devotees of funerals.
The dead man very soon was buried,
the priests and guests ate, drank, unhurried,
then each of them went on his way
as if he'd spent a useful day.
Our Eugene's now a rustic fellow,
the lord of workshops, waters, land,
of woods (he'd been a wastrel and
an enemy of order); mellowed
and glad his way of life has changed,
he now loves what had once seemed strange.

54

For two whole days it all was peerless,
secluded fields, a peaceful nook,
the cooling park, though dark and cheerless,
the bubbling of the quiet brook . . .
But by the third day groves and swallows,
the hills and meads, the charming hollows,
they couldn't hold him any more,
they bored him all, he quickly saw
that though there were no cards, no ditties,
no streets, no balls, no palaces,
the countryside both was and is
as dull and dreary as the city.
Ennui now seemed to fill his life,
pursued him like a faithful wife.

55

But I was born to an existence
of wild and rural solitude,
my lyre resounds with more insistence,
ideas are there in plenitude.
I dedicate myself to leisure,
stroll past a sheltered lake with pleasure
and *far niente* is my way.
For I am woken every day
to sweetest warmth, to utter freedom,
I read but little, sleep a lot,
all thought of fame is soon forgot.
Was this not like my former kingdom,
when in my blissful youth I stayed
recumbent, idle, in the shade?

56

Oh flowers, love, you fields and meadows,
Oh idleness, yours is my soul;
I'm not Eugene, we're different fellows,
that matters to me on the whole
in case some too sarcastic readers
or other bookish, slanderous creatures
should callously compare my quirks
with those of Byron and his works,
as if I were but merely scrawling
my effigy, just like that proud
fantast, as people put around
so shamelessly, (which I find galling),
as if we wrote of nothing else
but poems all about ourselves.

57

Now let me say in this connection,
all poets dream their loving dreams.
Some things which I hold in affection
emerge in fancy, where it seems
my soul preserves their secret image;
the muse then used them to advantage
and so my voice would carefree ring.
Of mountain maidens I would sing,
of my ideal, or also captives
upon the banks of the Salgir.
And you, my friends, I often hear
you ask: 'For whom, say, does your plaintive
affecting lyre sigh? Which maid
will now receive your accolade?

58

'Whose gaze, arousing inspiration,
rewarded your so pensive song,
caressing you? Whose adoration
are you attempting to prolong?'
But nobody's, my friends, believe me!
It was love's madness which deceived me,
as I forlornly was to learn . . .
How happy he who now can turn
the pains of passion into verses,
in Petrarch's steps he'll then be free
to pen exalted poetry,
and thus revoke his heart's reverses,
permitting fame at last to come,
yet I, in love, was numb and dumb.

59

Once love had passed, the muse then surfaced,
the darkness in my mind had cleared.
Now free, I seek again the sweetness
of magic sounds and thoughts that cheered.
I write, my heart no longer hurting,
my pen, entranced, is now averting
those doodles of girls' heads or feet
with verses as yet incomplete.
Extinguished ashes will not glimmer . . .
Although downcast, I shed no tears
and soon the storm will disappear,
within my silent soul will shimmer
the measures of an epic song
some five-and-twenty cantos long.

60

My story's plan has now been finished,
I've also found my hero's name.
This chapter's done, though not unblemished,
as I have found out to my shame.
The inconsistencies are many,
but I'll not change them, all or any,
I'll pay the censor what he's due
and then there are my critics, too,
devouring greedily my efforts.
Be off, then, to the Neva's banks,
my new-born work, now go and swank
and earn for me the tributes, plaudits
which I deserve, though you induce
bewilderment, alarm, abuse.

CHAPTER TWO

Oh rus!
    Horace
Oh Rus'!

CHAPTER TWO

1

The country place where Eugene languished
was thought by most a charming spot,
to which we'd all be gladly banished,
and be delighted with our lot.
The manor-house lay quite secluded,
from there the rough winds were excluded,
completely sheltered by a hill
above a river. In the still
remoteness hamlets lay, and meadows
with grazing herds upon the plain,
the fields aglow with golden grain;
a vast, neglected park cast shadows
where in the midday summer heat
the pensive Dryads could retreat.

2

The ancient house had been created
as houses of its sort should be,
built strong and finely decorated,
the taste of ancient ancestry.
The rooms had lofty, spacious ceilings,
were damask-hung and most appealing,
with forebears' portraits on the walls,
tiled stoves in all the rooms and halls.
Today such things are antiquated,
I really can't imagine why,
and anyway I won't deny
my friend found all this overrated,
for any room, both old or new
produced in him a yawn or two.

3

He chose a chamber in the chateau
in which the rural greybeard had
for forty years looked through the window
and driven his old servant mad
by squashing flies upon the curtain.
A simple room, the floor was oaken,
two cupboards, table, a divan,
no spots of ink, all spick and span.
Onegin opened both the cupboards
in which he found liqueurs, accounts,
and *eau-de-pomme* in large amounts;
from eighteen-eight there were some records –
the old man had no time to look
at any other sort of book.

4

Alone with all of his possessions,
and just to while the time away,
Onegin found a new obsession
with what his serfs were forced to pay.
Our backwoods sage and youthful hermit
decided he would strictly limit
how much each owed; his great idea
was rents which really weren't too dear.
Though this good fortune pleased the peasants,
one thrifty neighbour had a fit
and said no good would come of it,
another smiled but, sly, unpleasant,
they all of them were quite agreed
that he was dangerous indeed.

5

Initially they called to visit,
but when he heard a rustic coach
he had a Don horse, quite exquisite
and quick, brought round as they approached,
on which he fled before their advent.
Outraged that he was always absent,
they thought he was a dreadful boor,
so visitors grew ever fewer.
"Our neighbour is a frightful villain,
his actions wholly asinine,
drinks tumblers brimming with red wine,
won't kiss a lady's hand. A Mason!
Instead of 'No sir', 'Yes sir', says
offhandedly just 'No' and 'Yes'"!

6

Just then a young man made his entrance,
a landlord who had driven down
and also gave the neighbours substance
for gossip, questions and a frown.
The youth was called Vladímir Lenksi,
who'd come from Göttingen and whence he
from misty Germany had brought
a dream of freedom and Kant's thought;
a handsome chap and filled with learning,
he loved composing poems, too.
Impetuous, he was imbued
with passion, spirit and a burning
intensity, he spoke with flair,
had shoulder-length black curly hair.

7

The world's corruption had not withered
nor frozen hard his boyish verve,
which an attractive girl's come-hither,
a friend's 'hello' helped him preserve.
He was naïve concerning feelings,
his trust in hope made him appealing,
while modern life, ornate, uncouth,
impressed the mind of this fine youth.
Sweet transports of imagination
helped quell the doubts deep in his heart.
The purpose of our life, the part
we play, these fired his inspiration,
and with such things he racked his brains,
expecting wonders for his pains.

8

He felt there was a kindred spirit
just yearning to unite with him.
She waited every day, albeit
despondent, pining, on fate's whim.
He thought his friends were always ready
to sacrifice themselves, with steady,
unfailing hand defend his name
from any wicked slander's shame;
that there were some whom fate would favour,
those hallowed friends of all mankind,
immortals who would surely find
a way to make us see and savour
the radiance and happiness
with which the world might yet be blest.

9

Humanity and indignation
together with the love of Good,
the thought of fame brought him elation
and filled his boyhood, as they should.
His lyre in hand, he'd blithely wander
beneath the skies into the yonder
with Goethe, Schiller, soul aflame
with all their poetry and fame.
A carefree youth, he'd not discredit
the noble muses of his art,
nor in his songs would he depart
from his proud purpose as a poet,
the surging, virgin fantasy,
the charm of grave simplicity.

10

He sang of love, of love's surrender,
his song as lucent and as bright
as maidens' thoughts; like sleeping, tender
untroubled infants, like the light
of Luna in the wide horizons
of cloudless skies which she emblazons,
a goddess, the divinity
of moonlit nights and mystery.
He sang of sadness, separation,
of distant places, vacant sighs,
romantic roses, mackerel skies,
of *anything*, while desperation
at life's forever fading sheen
bedewed his eyes, at just eighteen.

11

The feasts thrown by his country neighbours
did not conform to Lenski's tastes;
Eugene alone admired his labours
of all the dwellers in those wastes.
So Lenski fled the noisy rabble
whose solemn and sagacious babble
of alcohol and making hay,
of kennels, kinsmen in no way
aroused poetic inspiration
or shone with wit, intelligence,
finesse, still less with common sense
or any cultured conversation.
And when their *wives* tried to converse,
they were, oh horror, even worse.

12

Good-looking, young and very wealthy,
extremely welcome everywhere,
in line with country custom, Lenski
is seen as someone to ensnare,
a husband for an unwed daughter,
this 'foreigner' which fate had brought her.
Whenever he drops in they gawk
discreetly and obliquely talk:
"How humdrum life is when one's single,"
then wander to the samovar,
as Mother fetches a guitar
and says: "My child, now go and mingle!"
The daughter starts to strum and bawl,
"Oh come into my golden hall . . ."

13

But Lenski had of course no craving
to tie himself in marriage bonds.
Instead he longed to meet Onegin,
(of whom he'd soon be very fond).
And so they shortly got together,
not in the least birds of a feather,
like verse and prose, or ice and flame,
or wave and stone, they weren't the same!
Initially each bored the other,
then friendship flowered and the two
went riding every day, and grew
inseparable like loving brothers,
friends forged – I'd be the first to say –
by doing nothing night and day.

14

But men today feel no affection,
each sees himself as number one,
the rest are naught, but *he's* perfection . . .
Thank God that attitude has gone,
Napoleons are all and sundry,
while those who're not are in a quandary,
mere underdogs, two-legged tools:
affection is the food of fools.
Eugene, however, more than many,
was tolerant, though knowing men,
he also often scoffed at them.
There were a few, and not just any,
whom he respected very much,
though with no sentiment as such.

15

He smiled at Lenski's lively chatter,
the poet's elevated fire,
his restless, buoyant youthful patter
and gaze eternally inspired.
All this was novel to Onegin,
who didn't criticise, stayed sanguine,
and thought: "I mustn't interfere
with his brief rapture, I won't sneer,
for he'll get over it without me,
so let him seek his happiness,
trust in the world's untaintedness,
and meanwhile live in peace, serenely,
so we'll forgive his ecstasy,
the glow of youth's intensity."

16

They both enjoyed their brisk discussions
and such ideas as they brought forth,
of long-gone states, their constitutions,
the fruits of learning and their worth,
old preconceptions, Good and Evil,
the sepulchre's mysterious riddle,
the sense of Life, the laws of Fate
were constant subjects of debate.
The poet's passionate contentions
led him in blissful reverie
to reel off Nordic poetry
which Eugene heard without dissension,
although he hardly understood
a single word, try as he would.

17

But passion haunted them more often,
obsessed my youthful eremites:
its hold on Eugene had now softened,
he spoke of it without delight
and grudgingly, though with contrition.
How happy he whose own volition
has freed him from that burning fire,
still happier he without desire,
his ardour cooled by separation,
by gossip, enmity and strife,
who's yawned and stretched with friends and wife,
released from jealous contemplation,
who has not squandered his estates
upon the two-faced two of spades.

18

When we have marched beneath the colours
of sage and calm tranquility,
when passion's flame has once been smothered
and now seems droll to you and me,
its wilfulness and heart-felt urgings,
its aftermath of sluggish surgings,
which are so taxing to restrain,
at times we like to entertain
ourselves by listening to a stranger's
tumultuous and then forthright
old anecdotes which can excite
our heart; just as an ageing soldier,
forgotten, eavesdrops when young braves
relate the dangers which they crave.

19

Regarding ardent adolescence,
it can't keep secret anything,
however joyful or unpleasant,
it quickly blurts out everything.
His love-life very inauspicious,
Eugene considered it delicious
as Lenski opened up his heart,
employing all the poet's art.
He had a chaste and upright conscience,
which he quite guilelessly laid bare,
Onegin found that he could share
his friend's naïve and heady nonsense,
emotions which, however true,
are not exactly all that new.

20

Ah, Lenski loved as no one ever
will love again today; alone
a poet's soul has strength and fervour
enough to love and suffer, groan
with ardour, grief, endure afflictions
incessantly without restriction,
one wish, one woe and constantly
one never-ending reverie!
So no amount of foreign beauties,
nor chilling distance, severance,
nor ages spent in deference
to muses, mirth, or learning's duties
had quashed in him an energy
sustained by pure vitality.

21

While still a lad he'd been enraptured
by Olga; though too young to know
the pangs of love, he'd yet been captured
by childish charms, and watched her grow.
He'd shared her callow games and pleasure,
they'd played in shaded parks together,
the children's fathers (who were friends)
had hoped they'd marry in the end.
Her parents lived in comfort, happy,
delighting in her radiance,
her flowering, pleasing innocence,
a hidden lily of the valley,
unseen, an unknown rarity
to either butterfly or bee.

22

She was the one who gave the poet
his first and greatest taste of joy
and thoughts of her inspired a sonnet
or music in the blissful boy.
So farewell, all you golden hours!
He learned to love the leafy bowers,
seclusion, stillness, night and moon,
the stars were his companions soon –
the moon, celestial light of darkness,
to which we used to dedicate
our evening walks, both early, late,
our tears, those comforters of sadness.
But now we only see in her
a dreary lamp, a mere poseur.

Obedient and always modest,
as merry as the morn, a miss
just like our poet, artless, honest,
enchanting as young love's first kiss;
her eyes were clear, bright blue in colour,
with flaxen locks, her smile a stunner,
her movements, voice and slender waist,
yes, Olga was enchanting, chaste,
a true . . . But study any novel
and you will find her portrait there.
I liked it once and thought it fair,
but now I think it's simply awful.
And so, my reader, we'll adjourn
and to her sister let us turn.

Tatiana was a little older:
this name has until now not graced
romantic prose, but we'll be bolder
and let it take its rightful place.
Why shouldn't we? It's full and pleasant,
though hardly known until the present,
unless from naughty night-time jaunts
to housemaids' private bedroom haunts.
Our taste in names is quite depressing
and, passing over Russian verse,
the French Enlightenment is worse:
we can't avoid, (how sad), admitting
that it has proved a dreary chore,
an affectation – nothing more!

25

So then, her name was Tatiana.
She neither had her sister's grace
nor Olga's cheerful girlish laughter,
the rosy freshness of her face,
she'd not attract admiring glances
at social gatherings or dances;
untamed and silent, sad and slow,
as timid as a sylvan doe,
a child herself amongst the others,
she never frolicked, played the clown,
nor ever wished to snuggle down,
embrace her father or her mother.
Instead she'd sit alone and still
while gazing by the window-sill.

26

Solemnity had been her partner
for nearly all her childhood days,
the rural life had beautified her
with daydreams in a leisured way.
Her delicate and slender fingers
were not inclined to ever linger
above some framed embroidery,
her needle lacked the mastery
to decorate the quilts and linen,
she only wished to dominate
her dolls: she taught them not to hate
decorum (as becomes young women),
and Mama's words, which she'd recite
until the doll had got them right,

27

but yet she never really troubled
to prattle, jabber, even play
with dollies, which she wouldn't cuddle
or dress in fashions of the day;
she thought all childish pranks too horrid,
for she loved most of all a torrid
and grisly tale on winter nights,
enthralling her till she took fright,
and when her loving nurse assembled
the other girls to skip and run,
Tatiana always was the one
who, unlike Olga, never gambolled,
but found the merriment and noise
intruded on her solemn poise.

28

She loved to wait upon Aurora
betimes upon her balcony,
to watch the singing stars before her
make way for daytime's euphony,
the heavens, hazy as they lighten,
as leisurely the background brightens,
the wafting wind, each morning's guide,
as dawn is fashioned from the night.
In winter when the dark possesses,
still drowsy, half the sleeping world,
the idle Orient is curled
in dreams, the misty moon's caresses
awakened her and she would rise
by candlelight to feast her eyes.

29

From early days she loved a novel,
they were her all, for them she glowed,
she read and then stayed staunchly loyal
to Richardson and to Rousseau.
Her father was a kindly fellow,
though out of touch and fairly shallow,
a man who'd never read a book,
so he was glad to overlook
his daughter's secrets which lay dozing
beneath her pillow while she slept.
Mere toys to him, he'd no respect
for either poetry or prose in
whatever guise, and yet his wife
loved Richardson as much as life.

30

Although the matron loved him dearly
she'd never read her Richardson,
nor was it that in fact she really
loathed Lovelace or prized Grandison.
But long ago Princess Alina,
a maiden cousin, when she'd seen her,
had often raved about the pair,
emotions which she longed to share.
Her troth was then already plighted,
though very much against her will,
she craved another and thus still
regretted him, her life was blighted:
her Grandison adored the cards,
a fop and Ensign in the Guards.

31

Like him, she always dressed according
to fashion, most becomingly.
Her parents, though, without a warning
betrothed her unexpectedly,
and so to quell her grievous sorrow
her husband drove her on the morrow
directly to his country seat,
where she was sadly made to meet
God only knows what sort of people.
She raged, she wept and almost forced
her husband to a quick divorce.
But soon she found the household vital,
for heaven makes us pleased with less,
which we consider happiness.

32

And habit soon assuaged the anguish
that nothing else could dissipate,
she came to see what soon would vanquish
her grief and help it to abate,
for through her work and in her leisure
she found a potent counter-measure:
she'd rule her husband and like that
at home she'd be a 'monocrat'.
Now everything was fine and balmy,
she pickled mushrooms, ran the farm,
a weekly bath afforded calm,
shaved serfs intended for the army,
then, if annoyed, she'd cuff a maid,
and all without her husband's aid.

33

A young girl's album, (not beneath her),
she'd sign in blood, and sometimes deign
to call 'Prashkovia' 'Paulina',
and speak in sing-song Moscow vein;
she'd worn a figure-crushing corset
which wouldn't fit unless she'd forced it,
her Russian 'N' was frenchified,
for she had learned to nasalize.
But soon all this no more amused her:
the corset, album, the Princess,
those verses full of mawkishness,
'Selina' now became 'Akulka'
and in the mornings she came down
in household cap and quilted gown.

34

And yet her husband loves her greatly,
he leaves her to get on with things,
relies on her in all innately,
relaxed with bathrobe, food and drink.
His life just rolls on, happy, homely,
some nights there is a small assembly
of kindly neighbours, simple friends,
who like to gather and unbend.
And so the evening quickly passes,
they chuckle over this and that,
or grumble or quite simply chat,
while Olga fetches tea and glasses.
Then supper comes and shortly, lo,
it's bedtime, and they have to go.

35

So life continued, calm and peaceful,
old customs were quite loyally
maintained, and pancakes made as usual
upon Shrove Tuesday, as should be.
They spent some time each year in fasting,
the serf-girls' simple songs and dancing
at Whitsun gladdened them as well,
as did the merry carousel.
And when in church during the service
the congregation yawned and prayed,
the Larins wept on their bouquet
and thought how very vital kvas is,
and afterwards their guests were served
as class and eminence deserved.

36

The pair at length became decrepit,
until the portal of the tomb
gaped wide and then received within it
her husband to its ghastly gloom,
on him a second crown bestowing.
He passed away, alone, unknowing,
before the midday meal was brought.
His family was overwrought,
the neighbours joined the lamentations,
though some were less than quite sincere.
A simple squire, he'd been revered,
his headstone bears the proclamation:
"Dimitri Larin, Brigadier,
Transgressor, Slave of God, Lies Here."

37

Now back among his household spirits
Vladímir Lenski quickly went
and paid his neighbour's grave a visit,
to sigh at this sad monument,
his heart unhappily aflutter.
"Alas, poor Yorick!" he then muttered,
and in a voice which was by turn
almost Shakespearean and Sterne,
"How often years ago he'd carry
me as an infant in his arms,
would let me touch without a qualm
his medal, and he hoped I'd marry
his Olga." Lenski felt that he
should write a gravestone threnody.

38

He tearfully then recollected
his parents' patriarchal dust,
whose memory he much respected.
How sad! Each generation must
enjoy a briefest harvest, flourish
upon fate's furrow, mellow, languish,
as providence's will dictates,
for next year's crop already waits.
And so our dizzy, flippant species
develops, hustles, bustles, raves,
and drags its forbears to the grave.
For us . . . for us the world soon ceases . . .
our grandsons, with no special fuss,
will one fine day get rid of us.

39

So let's enjoy it while we're able,
this giddy, merry life, my friends,
it's all a worthless, futile fable,
and of no value in the end.
I've closed my eyes to all illusions,
but sometimes distant hope's effusions
intrude upon my troubled heart:
I must confess that I would smart,
were I to leave this world forgotten.
I live, I write not for the praise,
but to exalt my dismal days
which have at least, at last, begotten,
just like a friend, my poetry,
preserving memories of me.

40

And someone's heart will be affected;
my verse, sustained by love and fate,
perhaps henceforth will be protected
from drowning in deep Lethe's spate.
Perchance — what abject expectation —
some future fool in veneration
will call the world's attention to
my portrait and, as is my due,
exclaim: "He really was a master!"
So please accept my heartfelt thanks,
my friends among the muses' ranks,
you who'll preserve my works hereafter,
whose loving hands will gently pet
an old man's laurel coronet.

CHAPTER THREE

Elle était fille; elle était amoureuse.
Malfilâtre

CHAPTER THREE

1

"You're going then? Oh dear, these poets!"
"Goodbye, Onegin, time I went."
"There's just one thing, I'd love to know it,
now, where are all your evenings spent?"
"The Larins' place." "That's terrifying,
the boredom must be stupefying.
Does it not seem a mindless crime
to spend your life in killing time?"
"No, not at all." "Well, there's a puzzle,
so let me tell you what I see:
a simple Russian family
which welcomes guests, which drinks and guzzles,
discusses jam and the delights
of rain and flax. Now am I right?"

2

" I don't quite see what's so appalling."
"The boredom is so bad, my boy!"
"I do not find your world enthralling,
a happy home's a source of joy
in which I can . . ." "Another idyll!
Enough my friend, oh damn and fiddle!
So now you're off, huh, that's a shame.
This Phyllis, Lenski – what's her name? -
of whom you babble, write and blubber,
please, could you think of any way
for both of us to meet one day?"
"You're joking!" "No." "You want to meet her?
O.K., but when?" "Right now." "That's great!
Then come with me, I've got a date!

3

Let's go!" And so the friends departed.
When they arrived they both received
a formal greeting, yet warm-hearted,
in which the Larins still believed,
observing all the old traditions;
preserves appeared, and in addition,
upon a table waxed to shine,
a jug brimful of fruity wine.
— — — — — — — — — — — — — — —
— — — — — — — — — — — — — — —
— — — — — — — — — — — — — — —
— — — — — — — — — — — — — — —
— — — — — — — — — — — — — — —
— — — — — — — — — — — — — — —

4

The friends then set off at a gallop.
They take the shortest route they can,
so let's be underhand and eavesdrop
on what they talk of, boy and man.
"Oh lord, Onegin, are you yawning?"
"A habit, Lenski." "Was it boring,
much more than normal?" "Just the same.
Oh look, the fields . . . now that's a shame,
they're getting darker. Well then, coachman,
it's dreadful here, so let's be gone.
That Mrs. Larin, she's a one,
a simple, charming, worthy woman,
although her wine, I rather fear,
will cost my stomach pretty dear.

5

But tell me, which was Tatiana?"
"Oh, she's the one who silently
came in and then, just like Svetlana,
sat by the window gloomily."
"How come you love the younger daughter?"
"Why not?" "A poet really ought to
have picked the other. Olga's like
some lifeless virgin by van Dyck.
She's round and fair of face, her features
are like the silly moon on high
embellishing the stupid sky."
Vladímir thought of the sweet creature,
and nodded curtly. What he'd heard
ensured he didn't speak a word.

6

Onegin's sudden apparition
at Larins' made on one and all
a quite spectacular impression.
Excited neighbours came to call,
they soon indulged in furtive prattle,
conjecture mixed with tittle-tattle,
they joked and judged with gleeful spite
if Tanya's prospects were now bright.
And there were those who then confided
they knew the secret wedding date,
but that the pair were forced to wait
until a ring could be provided.
But Lenski's marriage, people said,
would certainly soon go ahead.

7

Tatiana was exasperated
by all the gossip of this sort,
though secretly she was elated
and could not ban it from her thoughts.
She wasn't able to stop thinking,
indeed the feeling was now sinking
into her heart – fate had decreed
she was in love. Just as the seed
that falls to earth is brought to flower
encouraged by the warmth of spring,
thus Tanya had been wondering,
consumed with yearning's urgent power,
had craved the food of love, and so
she waited sadly . . . for her beau.

8

Her wait was soon rewarded. Gasping,
her eyes agape, she sighed, "It's him!"
Obsessed, she lay there, tortured, asking . . .
Her chance of sleep was pretty slim,
for all around she felt his presence,
as if some magic brought his essence
to the dear girl. The flattery
of friends annoyed her rapidly,
as did the glances of the servants.
She seemed a victim of despair,
the guests disturbed her everywhere,
their laziness aroused resentment,
and when they, without warning, called
to lounge about, she was appalled.

9

With what attention Tanya browses
in tender and diverting books;
seductive fiction now arouses
in her enchanted, longing looks!
The harvests of imagination
are vital, passionate creations:
the lover of Julie Wolmar,
Malek-Adhel and de Linar,
and Werther, sadly martyred, tragic,
the marvellous, matchless, Grandison,
whom *we* now find so wearisome,
for our young dreamer they were magic,
confused and fused, they were the same:
Onegin was the vision's name.

10

She now believes that she is truly
those heroines she's long adored:
Clarissa, Delphine, lovely Julie,
and so she roams alone abroad
through spacious peaceful woodlands, bearing
a novel which she thought was daring.
In it she seeks and finds, it seems,
a secret glow, and coyly dreams
of blissful passion, sweet and deathless . . .
She sighs, and having made her own
another's joy, another's groans,
she whispers in a trance, quite breathless,
a letter meant for . . . we shall see!
Not Grandison, take that from me!

11

There was a time when ardent poets
attuned their style to give it weight:
the hero was, (the bard would show it),
perfection in its pristine state:
to free a maiden was his duty,
of course she'd be a dazzling beauty,
intelligent, evocative,
her soul uniquely sensitive;
the hero cast aside all caution,
was fearless, eager, in a trice
prepared for any sacrifice,
and when we reach the final portion
we see how Evil is done down,
while Virtue gets its well-earned crown.

12

Yet nowadays our minds are lazy,
we love a novel full of vice;
morality is grown too hazy
and wickedness considered nice.
The British Muse's specious fables
result in young girls quite unable
to sleep at night, as they revere
Ahasver there and Sbogar here
or Melmoth (that unhappy vagrant),
the pensive Vampire, the Corsair:
Lord Byron never could forbear
by means of tricks, as apt as flagrant,
to turn his wretched self-esteem
into a glum romantic dream.

13

But where, my friends, is all this leading?
Perhaps a change will come on me,
a demon who, at heaven's pleading,
will make me give up poetry,
and having scorned the threats of Phoebus,
I'll write but prose of humble genus,
a novel of the old design
will help me cope with my decline.
There'll be no menacing depictions
of secret plots and villainy;
a simple Russian family
will be the subject of my fiction,
with darling dreams of love which glow
and tales of forebears long ago.

14

I'll chronicle the words of fathers,
an aged uncle's thoughtful looks,
describe the children who would rather
play under lime-trees by a brook,
distressing jealousy and torments,
or rifts and meetings, tearful moments.
The pair will have another spat,
there'll be a wedding after that.
I shall recount the fervid swooning
of lovers' words and lovers' ways
which I too loved in bygone days
when I was always busy mooning
around a girl and having fun,
but that was then, when I was young.

15

Tatiana, you're so young and vibrant,
both you and I can gently mourn,
because a modish, trendy tyrant
controls your fate . . . So be forewarned,
my dear, you'll doubtless be rejected;
till then there'll be some unexpected
euphoria, you'll feel the fire
of passionate, unquenched desire.
Where hope bedazzles, daydreams follow,
and everywhere will seem to you
just perfect for a rendezvous,
yes, all around, twixt hill and hollow,
take care, behind, before, beware,
you'll see your tempter everywhere.

16

The throes of love, its pain and ardour,
see Tanya brooding in the grounds,
a sudden languor makes it harder
for her to stroll and glance around;
her bosom heaves, her cheeks then redden,
the breath upon her lips soon deadens,
there is a shimmer in her eyes,
her ears are roaring, fading skies
grow dark, the moon begins its duty,
patrolling heaven's lofty vault,
the nightingale declines to halt
its mellow song of dulcet beauty;
for Tanya, sleepless, things get worse,
and so she whispers to her nurse:

17

"I still can't sleep, Nurse, it's so stifling,
unlatch the window, sit with me."
"What ails you, Tanya?" "Life's so trifling,
oh, tell me how it used to be."
"Well, what about it? I've forgotten
as good as everything, it's rotten
how much has gone. Though once I knew
all sorts of tales, and all were true,
of dreadful sprites and tragic maidens,
my memory's now very bad,
oh, Tanya, dear, it's all so sad,
I easily could be mistaken."
"Oh, Nurse, please tell me, if you can,
if you have ever loved a man?"

18

"Oh, young girls of my generation,
sweet Tanya, didn't know a thing,
for love entailed humiliation,
your ears were boxed – and did they ring!"
"How did you marry then?" "But Tanya,
I'm sure God willed it so. My Vanya
was younger than myself, my dear,
and I was barely thirteen years
of age. For some two weeks a broker
arranged it all and finally
he got my father to agree.
I wept with fear at my departure,
but then my pigtails were untied,
I went to church, came out a bride.

19

And then I went to foreign people . . .
But Tanya, you're not listening! . . ."
"Oh, Nurse, dear Nurse, I feel so feeble,
I'm sick at heart, you dear old thing!
and in despair; I'm almost crying . . ."
"My child, you're ill, you're surely dying,
the Lord have mercy on us all!
What shall I do? Oh, please don't bawl!
Here, let me sprinkle holy water
on you, you're ill, you're burning hot!"
"It's not like that, but what I've got
is, well . . . I think, oh Nurse . . . I'm sort of . . .
in love." The nurse prayed quickly and
then stroked her with a wrinkled hand.

20

"In love . . ." she whispered, devastated,
repeatedly to the old crone.
"My dearest girl, you're quite prostrated!"
"In love, in love! Leave me alone!"
The moon beamed darkly in the meantime,
engulfing with its murky moonshine
Tatiana's charms, so pale and fair,
her lovely, loose and flowing hair,
her teardrops and, upon a settle,
the aged crone by Tanya's bed,
a kerchief on her hoary head,
her body covered, warm and muffled.
Thus nurse and maiden dozed off soon
beneath a poignant, touching moon.

21

Her heart and mind began to wander,
then gradually a thought was born
while gazing at the moon up yonder
which left her feeling weak and torn.
"Please leave me, Nurse, you needn't stay there,
I beg you, fetch me pen and paper,
and push the table nearer here,
I'll be in bed soon, never fear . . .
Good night!" The heavens softly glimmer,
Tatiana, pensive, starts to write
a letter by the moon's pale light,
through which our Eugene's shadow shimmers.
Adoring flights of fancy soar,
but who's the finished letter for?

22

I've known some belles who were stand-offish,
unfeeling, cold, and winter-chaste,
relentless, moral, even snobbish,
inscrutable, with perfect taste.
I've marvelled at their self-importance
and at their virtuous forbearance,
and to be frank, I fled in dread!
It seemed to me that I had read
upon their brows the proclamation:
"Abandon hope for evermore,"
for love is all that they abhor
and frightening folks their recreation.
Perhaps upon the Neva's banks
you've seen them in their serried ranks.

23

And then there are those skittish women
surrounded by their willing beaus,
conceited, cold into the bargain,
and nonchalant from top to toe.
But yet to my unfeigned amazement
I found that their austere appraisement
which terrified the timorous,
could also, truly hideous,
attract them *back* again. Compassion,
it would appear, was how they drew
the men into their claws anew:
a tender word, precisely rationed,
ensured the lover could not see
the vagaries of vanity.

24

So why is Tanya, then, more guilty?
Because she's free of all deceit,
has acted lovably and simply
and been naïvely indiscreet?
Because we find her love appealing,
begotten of her deepest feelings?
Because she is ingenuous,
because she's been impetuous,
endowed with free imagination,
intelligence, a lively will,
a loving heart she cannot still,
rebellious anticipation?
Would you condemn a girl to hell
who's loved not wisely, but too well?

25

Whereas coquettes will reason coolly,
Tatiana's ardour is intense,
her adoration's absolutely
authentic and without pretence.
She's not the sort who says: Postpone it,
dissemble, fake, and then disown it,
intensify your lovers' throes,
relieving frenzied, frantic woes;
encourage them to make them zealous,
expectant; after that dismay
their hearts with mischief, and next day
revive the fires to make them jealous,
then leave them with their mouths agape
before they're able to escape.

26

There's one more problem I see waiting:
to save the honour of our land,
I sadly can't avoid translating
Tatiana's letter; as it stands,
the thing's in French. The Russian language
was strange to her, she couldn't manage
to read or understand the news,
express or scribble down her views;
she wrote in French, as was the fashion.
What can one do! For I repeat
a lady's love, however sweet,
has never been expressed in Russian.
As yet our proud and lovely tongue
is thought too coarse by old and young.

27

I know of those who'd make the ladies
learn Russian: quite grotesque, absurd!
They couldn't read (the idea's crazy!)
a weekly journal word for word!
It's you, my peers and fellow writers,
that I appeal to, you're the blighters
who, expiating all your sins,
have written secret, tender hymns
to doting damsels, who but poorly
pronounce our tongue and garble it
when trying out their sparkling wit;
My friends, I'm certain that you've surely
observed how soon a foreign tongue
becomes their normal, 'native' one.

28

The Lord prevent me ever meeting
a female egghead at a ball,
or lady pedants always bleating
and covered by a yellow shawl!
I can't stand Russian which emerges
from sullen lips with scarlet splurges
and free from any dire mistakes.
Perhaps — the notion makes me quake —
the ladies of a generation
who've trained on trivial gazettes
will charm us with their Grammar yet,
write verses worth consideration.
But I . . . My friends, why should I care?
For I will stick with standard fare!

29

The faulty and fallacious chatter,
the negligent misuse of words,
induce my heart to pit- and patter,
when listening to those mocking birds.
I see no need to heed the errors,
the Gallicisms cause no terrors,
to me they are still very dear,
just like my sins of yesteryear,
or Bógdanóvich's slight verses.
But that will do! The moment's here
for me to concentrate on dear
Tatiana's letter. *Now*? Yes, curse it!
But lacking Parny's tender vein,
I'd gladly spare myself the pain.

30

I'd love to ask dear Baratinski,
my friend and author of *The Feasts*,
were he but willing and still with me,
if his poetic gifts at least
could give a lovesick girl's confessions
enchanting, elegant expression.
Oh, come, my friend, where are you now?
I'll give my rights up with a bow!
But he is gone and wanders lonely
amidst a waste of dismal rocks
and cheerless, gloomy icy blocks
beneath the Finnish sky; if only
he somehow shared my vapid woe,
of which he sadly cannot know.

31

Tatiana's letter lies before me,
I guard it quite religiously;
to glance at it can overawe me,
yet I peruse it constantly.
Who taught her all that warm affection,
that charming verbal imperfection?
Who trained her in that touching tosh,
with heartfelt gossip all awash,
both dangerous and fascinating?
Where did she learn it? No idea!
The feeble version you'll find here
is what I've spent some time translating,
Like *Freischütz* played by some young chit
whose fingers cannot cope with it.

Tatiana's Letter to Onegin

I'll be so bold and send this letter.
What else is there that I should say?
To not have written might be better,
(you can reject me any day).
A hapless girl, you'll not forget her,
has written this and if you feel
one drop of pity, you'll not steal
away and leave me quite neglected.
At first I didn't want to write:
if once a week I'd but caught sight
of you while strolling, calm, collected,
to call on us, if I had talked
to you, or listened as we walked,
had been allowed to think and ponder
about one thing all night and day
till some fresh crossing of our ways,
would shame have stopped me, I now wonder?
But you're unsociable, it's said,
yet though you'd find us plain and humdrum –
it's true, we're simple and unread –
you'd always get the warmest welcome.

Why ever did you come to call?
Here in our little backwoods village
I know we'd not have met at all.
I never would have felt such anguish,
youth's turmoil would by then have vanished,
subdued by time and age – who knows-
I would have come across another,
become a worthy, loving mother,
a faithful wife, and found repose.

Another! . . . No one else has riven,
so touched or moved my heart before;
all this has been decreed by heaven,
a higher council: I am yours!
My every day has been a token
that I would see you very soon.
I know that God has really spoken:
you'll be my guardian to the tomb . . .

Before we met you were a vision,
already you were all to me,
your glance suffused me languorously,
your voice became my soul's possession.
It was no dream, I quickly knew,
and feeling faint, scarce had you entered,
I burned with passion and, tormented,
my mind cried out: "It's you! It's you!"

Oh, was it your voice in the distance
which in the stillness spoke to me,
when I would give the poor assistance,
as sorrow weakened my resistance,
and only prayer could set me free?
Was it not you who at that moment
appeared to me, adoring, ardent,
who slipped in through the limpid night
to lean across my sleeping figure?
Was it not you, with love and pleasure,
who whispered words of hope and light?
Who are you then? My guardian angel?
My tempter, and a faithless wastrel?
I beg of you, please soothe my qualms,
perhaps it's all just dull delusion,
a young girl's simple false alarms,
a trick of fate to cause confusion . . .

But so be it! I place my fate
into your hands for its safekeeping,
for your compassion plead and wait . . .
imagine me before you, weeping,
remember that I'm here alone,
for me there is no consolation,
my mind is wild with desperation,
in death alone can I atone.
So now I'll wait for your decision,
it only takes a single glance
to cause my heart to sing and dance
or break in two at your derision!

Farewell! I fear to read this through,
feel faint, distraught with shame and terror,
I trust your honour, trust in you,
for I am yours alone, forever.

32

By turns Tatiana sighs and mutters,
the letter trembles in her hand,
and as she licks the wafer, shudders,
her tongue as dry as desert sand.
Her head inclines towards her shoulder,
there is no nurse nearby to scold her,
the night-gown slips and so reveals
more shoulder as the moonlight steals
away, and through the mists the hollows
appear, and in a little while
the silver stream begins to smile;
the herdsman's strident horn soon follows
and wakes the village. Morning's there,
though Tanya simply doesn't care.

33

She doesn't notice that it's daybreak
and sits, her head upon her breast,
subdued and overwhelmed by heartache,
forgets to fix the waxen crest
upon her letter; *Nyanya*, softly,
unlocks the door and enters, gently
exclaiming as she brings the tea:
"You're well again! Oh, glory be!
But why, my dear, you're up so early!
I was upset, got such a fright
when you were in a fret last night.
It's wonderful, my early birdie!
You haven't even been to bed
and yet your face is poppy-red!"

34

"Oh *Nyanya* dear, do me a favour."
"Of course, my darling, just say how!"
"You mustn't think . . . oh please don't waver . . .
you really can't . . . refuse me . . . now."
"My dear, trust me, by God, completely."
"Well, send your grandson quite discreetly
to take this little note to O . . .
that neighbour . . . well, I mean . . . you know . . .
And tell the boy that he must never
divulge my name or mention me,
that he must set off secretly,
not say a word, not now . . . not ever."
"To *whom*? I've long lost count, my dear,
there are so many neighbours here."

35

"Oh Nurse, you really are slow-witted!"
"My dearest heart, I'm now so old,
my mind is dull, may God have pity,
there was a time, when I'd been told,
I knew at once what was expected . . ."
"Oh *Nyanya*, are your wits affected,
what are you going on about?
I simply cannot make you out!
Just listen now! You see, I'm talking
of this, a letter I must send
Onegin." "Dear, I'll make amends,
yes, now I see . . . my mind's not working . . .
You're pale again!" "Oh never mind,
now send your grandson, be so kind."

36

The day departs, and then another,
she waits, but still there's no reply;
so, sad and pale, she tries to smother
her fears, and not to weep or sigh.
A man appears, but she discovers
that it is only Olga's lover.
"Oh, tell me please, but where's your friend?"
her mother asks as he descends,
"It seems he wants to keep his distance!"
Tatiana quivers, hears him say,
"He said he'd be along today,
he's writing letters – such a nuisance!"
Tatiana gazes at the ground,
as if she's heard a vulgar sound.

37

Then night-time neared, and softly gleaming
the samovar warmed up the tea
inside the pot and, gently steaming,
the vapours wafted lazily.
As Olga poured the fragrant liquid
a footman, for the job conscripted,
helped out, and as the dusky stream
poured forth, he then poured in the cream.
Tatiana stood before the window
and breathed upon the frosty pane,
then, lost in dreams, she sighed again,
and when she saw the misty shadow,
the young girl's finger, grave and slow,
roughed out the letters E and O . . .

38

And all the time her soul is yearning,
her anxious gaze is filled with tears.
Hoofs thud! Her worried face is burning,
as on a horse Eugene draws near . . .
and stops outside. Ah! Tanya scurries
excited, phantom-like, she hurries
first through the hall, the porch, then straight
into the garden, doesn't wait,
but flies and flees, yet never glances
behind her, for she does not dare;
she's crossed the lawn, a bridge, a stair,
pushed through the lilacs, then she prances
across the flower-beds, retreats
till, panting, she espies a seat

39

on which she rests. "He's here! Onegin
has come! Good God, what must he think!"
Her hope-filled heart finds it dismaying,
and anguish makes her cheeks glow pink.
She waits aghast, her ears are ringing.
What will he do? The maids are singing,
but Tanya cannot hear or see;
the girls are chanting by decree
while plucking berries in the garden
(to stop them if they want to munch
their master's berries for their lunch,
as singing makes it so much harder:
there is no way to sing *and* eat,
a cunning rural mental feat).

Song of the Girls

Maidens, pretty maidens all,
darling girls, it's you we call,
romp quite freely one and all,
have your fling, and run or sprawl,
join with us and sing our ditty,
sing our ditty, blithe and pretty,
catch yourselves a charming boy,
let him share your song and joy!

When you see a passing lad,
make him yours and don't be sad,
then we'll pluck and scatter berries,
pelt the lad with crimson cherries,
currants, fruits of every kind,
anything that we can find.

Don't approach and don't come near us,
never try to overhear us,
never try to find our names,
Don't disturb our girlish games.

40

Tatiana heard them, quite indifferent
to singing servants and their song,
she waited, nervous and impatient
and hoped for peace before too long,
and yet her breast remained atremble,
her blushing cheeks indeed resembled
a fire; they burned more brightly still,
just like, imagine if you will,
a roguish schoolboy's wretched capture:
a flashing, brilliant butterfly
which can't escape, nor flutter by . . .
a hunted hare that hides and, trapped there
in winter grass, then tries to run
from huntsmen coursing with their guns.

41

So finally she rose and, sighing,
began to wander thoughtfully
along the verdant pathway lying
before her, when she suddenly
saw Eugene, eyes ablaze and awesome,
just like a dreadful shade, as if some
corrosive flame had struck and burned
her, stopping Tanya as she turned.
Today, however, my dear reader,
I lack the strength to carry on
recounting what occurred upon
their meeting; truth to tell, I need a
few moments merriment and rest,
if you would see me at my best.

CHAPTER FOUR

La morale est dans la nature des choses.
Necker

CHAPTER FOUR

1–6
7

The less a woman's shown affection,
the greater seems her love for us
and so much easier her seduction,
which can be brought off without fuss.
Time was, when every form of lewdness
was not considered shameless rudeness,
but lauded as a kind of art
and bragged about, as though a part
of making merry, without passion.
Yet this amusing sort of jape
is only suited to an ape
from when our forebears were in fashion;
no one today would give a fig,
for Lovelace, crimson shoes or wig.

8

Who is not bored with constant posing,
repeating endlessly the same,
persuading people by proposing
what others have for years proclaimed;
encountering the same objections,
eradicating misconceptions
which never, now or then, have been
believed by damsels of thirteen?
And who by now has not grown weary
of threats, entreaties, bogus fear,
of lengthy notes and insincere
laments, deceptions, and the leery
surveillance of their mothers, aunts,
the friendships which their husbands grant?

9

That's what Eugene believed exactly,
for in the first flush of his youth
he'd known great ardour and in fact he'd
at times appeared almost uncouth.
This way of life had left him pampered:
one day his pleasures were unhampered,
the next he was intensely tired
of things which he had just desired,
fed up with all his cheap successes,
oblivious to peace or noise,
his soul began to lose its poise
and yawning's now how he suppresses
a laugh; it's not too much to say
that he has thrown eight years away.

10

No longer is he always smitten;
he's now content to cast around,
and if a fish has not soon bitten,
his suffering is not profound.
He's wooing women without fervour
and, parting from them without rancour,
forgets forthwith their love and spite,
just as a blasé caller might
arrive to join an evening party
of whist, sit down, then when the hand
is over, call his carriage and
put on his coat, replete and hearty,
go home to sleep, without a clue
what day will bring, or what he'll do.

11

But when he read Tatiana's missive
Onegin was quite deeply stirred;
the young girl's language seemed so pensive
as he reflected on her words;
he then recalled the lovely dreamer's
anaemic look and sad demeanour
and, in a trance-like reverie,
imagined her pure honesty.
Perhaps the fires of former feelings
possessed him briefly once again,
yet he had no desire to pain
an innocent he found appealing.
But let us to the meeting flit
and see how Tanya copes with it.

12

Now for a second both are silent;
then Eugene takes a step or two
in her direction, halts a moment,
and says: "You wrote to me. It's true,
for I have read your soul's confessions,
a blameless heart's intense professions.
Your openness is dear to me,
for it has set emotions free
which have for years been muddled, stranded.
It's not to praise I'm here today,
my only wish is to repay
your frankness; I'll be just as candid
and speak the truth, which I'll not fudge,
and you yourself can be my judge.

13

"Had I the wish to be a husband,
a father, lead a quiet life,
bestowed on me by fortune, just and
benign, with family and wife,
if I found house and home attractive,
if ever I could be their captive,
then I would take the greatest pride
in asking you to be my bride.
I say this without affectation,
in you I've found my lost ideal
and would have chosen you, I feel,
alone as perfect consolation
in my declining, gloomy days,
and still been happy in some ways.

14

"I sadly say upon reflection
that I'm not made for happiness,
I do not merit your perfection,
unsuited by unworthiness.
It's on my mind, take my assurance,
we'd both be bored beyond endurance,
if we were fool enough to wed.
I'd soon be sick of you, I'd dread
to see you weep, although your weeping
would not affect or move my heart,
but just enrage me; I'd depart.
Such are the roses Hymen's keeping
to strew in front of you and me,
for months and years quite probably.

15

"What in the world could be more awful
than some poor wife who waits up late
and all alone, her husband woeful
and worthless, cursing cruel fate
in spite of his wife's countless merits,
a man who's silent, in low spirits,
yet jealous, always cross and cold,
like me? Was it for this your soul
aspired and burned, when you so dearly
and yet so simply wrote to me?
Was it for this that you felt free
to say what you said oh so clearly?
You surely cannot wish it true
that such a fate's reserved for you!

16

"Past dreams and years are past repealing,
my soul can never be renewed;
I love you with a brother's feeling,
perhaps a little more. If you'd
now hear me please, without displeasure:
a girl will often learn to treasure
a dream, and then another one,
as saplings in the balmy sun
with each new spring replace their foliage,
for this, it seems, has been ordained;
you'll love again . . . But be restrained
in what you do and in your language.
A stranger would be shocked, you know,
and inexperience leads to woe."

17

That's how Onegin gave his sermon.
Tatiana listened through her tears,
said nothing, she was almost broken
as he confirmed her direst fears.
He offered her his arm, and bravely
she leaned on it as they both gravely,
('mechanically' as we would say),
meandered onward, she *distraite*,
around the kitchen garden, homeward;
when both of them had reached the house
no outraged passions were aroused,
as no one felt that they'd been forward,
for country folk don't make a fuss,
no more than haughty Moscow does!

18

I'm sure that you'll agree, dear reader,
our friend has acted properly
towards poor Tanya; he reveals here
once more his true nobility,
though people's spite and frank ill-feeling
combined to leave our hero reeling,
for whether foe or whether friend
(there's not much difference in the end),
they vilified him without mercy.
We all have rivals here and there,
it's friends of whom we should beware,
for they're the ones who can turn nasty.
Ah me! Those friends, those friends! I sigh
as I recall them. I know why!

19

What's that? Oh, nothing! I'm just quelling
contemptible and morbid thoughts;
yet *en passant* I can't help telling
you, one and all, that there is nought,
no slander which is not too shameful,
or foolishness, however hateful,
which some immoral reprobate
among the mob won't hesitate
to spread, no epigram too silly
for friends to constantly repeat,
without real malice or conceit
of course, they do it willy-nilly
and all the time they will profess
they're treating you like kin, no less!

20

So, gentle reader, are your kindred
all absolutely fit and well?
Forgive me if I am quite candid,
perhaps you won't mind if I tell
you something touching your relations,
your 'kinsfolk' and their expectations?
So here's what 'kindred' really means:
we are expected to esteem
and flatter them, to show affection;
then duty calls us once a year
to visit them, bring Christmas cheer,
according to the old conventions;
and then we hope to be ignored . . .
A lengthy life be their reward!

21

And as for all those lovely ladies,
their love surpasses that of kin
or friend, for whilst the storm still rages
it follows us through thick and thin.
That's true, no doubt! But then there's fashion
and also nature's wayward passions,
the floods of thought which nothing checks . . .
And don't forget the fairer sex,
as light as fluff, whose husband's interests,
should deferentially be prized
by virtuous obedient wives:
that's how your loving, faithful mistress
could vanish in a cloud of smoke,
for Satan loves a fiendish joke!

22

Who *can* we trust, then? And who treasure?
On whom can *you* alone rely?
Our words, our deeds, who's there to measure
them all, and then to justify
what we have done by our own yardstick?
Who don't we find too soporific?
Who cossets us with every care?
Who never smears us anywhere?
Who doesn't find our vices dreadful?
Instead of following the trail
of someone chasing his own tail,
act in a way which is more useful.
Dear reader, here is what to do!
The one to love is namely – you!

23

What was the outcome of the meeting?
Alas! It's not too hard to guess!
Tatiana's youthful heart is beating
with agitation, shock; obsessed
with sadness, no, it's really rather
a more intense and joyless ardour
with which our poor Tatiana burns;
she cannot sleep, she tosses, turns,
her health, life's sweetness and its flower,
her smile, her modest, wholesome peace
had, like an empty sound, quite ceased,
her youthful soul appeared to glower,
just as a storm that's on the way
will blacken the approaching day.

24

And so Tatiana slowly weakens,
grows pale, then dwindles, and is still;
she's lost all interest, hardly eaten,
her soul is dead, as is her will.
The neighbours shake their heads quite gravely,
and whisper to each other sagely:
high time indeed that she was wed . . .
But there's no more that need be said.
I'll hurry now to raise your spirits
and paint a scene of happiness;
instinctively, I must confess
that pity sadly shows my limits:
forgive me, please, for I adore
my dear Tatiana more and more!

25

The charms of Olga quickly captured
young Lenski's heart, complete and whole;
before too long he was enraptured
and joyfully gave up his soul.
He's always there, and sits together
with her in darkened rooms; whenever
they can, they wander, arm in arm,
around the lawns without a qualm.
And what of it? Intoxicated
with love, confused by tender shame,
he coyly murmurs her sweet name,
encouraged by her smile, elated
he kisses trimmings on her dress
or plays with some loose, flowing tress.

26

At times he reads aloud a story,
some novel of a moral brand,
whose author painted nature's glory
much better than Chateaubriand;
and every now and then he shyly
omits some deviation, slyly
leaves out a passage which he thought
unsuitable and of the sort
a tender maiden should beware of . . .
and far away from one and all
they play at chess, both quite enthralled,
while Lenski, spellbound, unaware of
his actions, doesn't really look
and takes his pawn with his own rook!

27

He then drives home. Until the morning
she's in his thoughts and fills his dreams;
he spends a happy hour adorning
her album with assorted scenes:
some rustic views, a temple, gravestone,
a dove (all lightly coloured), high-flown
romantic verse on other leaves
beneath some names which interweave
with other signatures and couplets
in garlands filled with poesy,
those tranquil shrines of reverie,
enduring testaments or trinkets:
a moment's thought was thus arranged
in such a way, and never changed.

28

You have, of course, at times encountered
a young girl's album where her friends
from country houses all around her
have scrawled their names from end to end;
defying normal rules of spelling,
they pen disjointed verses telling
of friendship's pleasures and delights
in rhythms which are never right.
Upon the first page you will notice
Qu'écrirez-vous sur ces tablettes?
initialled: *toute à vous Annette*;
the album starts thus, and it closes:
"*By hook, by crook, now take a look,
my name's the last one in the book!*"

29

Two hearts, a torch, and diverse flowers
are what you'll find on every page,
and also rhymes about the powers
of love "*from now until the grave*";
or maybe something even bolder,
the work of some 'poetic' soldier.
My friends, I too am glad to draft
a poem, and however daft,
for such an album, since I'm sure that
my trash would nonetheless receive
acclaim; what's more, I do believe
that no one would be keen to sneer at
what I have scrawled, or study it
for signs of subtlety and wit.

30

And as for all you sundry volumes,
escaped from Satan's library,
magnificent and noble albums
which plague our bards so gleefully,
with painters' brush-work illustrated,
and poets' verses decorated,
may God's damnation strike you down!
I always have to hide a frown
when fine and splendid ladies offer
in-quarto albums for a verse;
within my soul a waspish curse
begins to bite, but I can't proffer
the epigram which it has stirred –
for they would not be genteel words.

31

But Lenski proffers more than phrases
in Olga's album, when he can;
his pen breathes love and sings her praises –
no frigid wit comes from this man!
Extolling Olga's worth and spirit,
his adoration knows no limit,
and what he hears and what he sees
he fashions into elegies,
like you, Yazikov; your exalted,
inspiring songs to God knows whom,
your elegies, those poignant blooms
which, once they have all been collected,
will form a perfect narrative
of all you were and how you lived.

32

Hang on! Have you not heard? The critic,
exacting, stern, has ordered us
to throw away our wretched, tragic
and elegiac wreaths. "Don't fuss,
stop going on about what's finished,
what time and chance have long diminished;
enough's enough, you dated bards,
you really shouldn't find it hard
to sing of something else!" "How valid
your judgement is! You will, no doubt,
point out what we should write about:
revive the dagger, mask and trumpet,
is that what we should now compose?"
"What rubbish! Write majestic odes,

33

"such as an earlier age created,
a grander age, in times of yore!"
"Majestic odes?" "They're venerated!"
"Come on, come on, whatever for?
They're all the same! Have you forgotten
the satirist and what he's written?
Do you prefer that shrewd and smart
lampoon of lyrists and their art,
As Others See It, to our rhymers,
however feeble?" "Elegies
are tame and dull; they do not please,
while odes are altogether finer . . ."
But I will stop this now before
two epochs find themselves at war!

34

What odes might Lenski not have fashioned!
By fame and freedom overawed,
his thoughts and feelings were impassioned,
but odes left Olga feeling bored.
Don't tearful poets always relish
the chance to read to those they cherish?
It's said there is no greater prize,
so happy they who rhapsodise,
those modest lovers raptly gazing
while reading reveries out loud,
rejoicing as their words resound,
to languid, tender beauties lazing . . .
although the thoughts of these same belles
might easily be somewhere else.

35

But I recite the fruits of musing,
my dulcet and harmonious verse,
to one who always finds it soothing,
that partner of my youth – my nurse;
or after dinner I'll belabour
some hapless, apathetic neighbour
who's rashly strayed within my grasp,
whose fleeing coat-tails I can clasp
and sit him choking in a corner,
so I can mouth a tragedy;
yet, jokes apart, when poetry
subdues me and I sadly wander
beside the lake, my honeyed words
are sure to frighten off the birds.

36/37

What of Eugene? I crave your patience,
dear brothers, for a little bit,
I'll just describe his occupations
in detail for your benefit.
Onegin's life was quite secluded,
and when in summer it was humid
he rose at six and, lightly dressed,
set off towards a stream with zest,
which flowed beneath a nearby hillock;
Byronic, he'd then swim across
this Hellespont and then be off
back home to dress and warm his stomach
with coffee, read some rag . . . . . .
. . . .

38/39

A ramble, sleeping soundly, reading,
the shady woods, the burbling streams,
and every now and then succeeding
in snatching kisses, unforeseen,
from pretty, dark-eyed girls, a fiery
but well-trained horse, good wine, a really
congenial dinner, and his peace,
and quiet, solitude, release –
Onegin's life was thus quite blameless,
surrendering in every way
to countless warm and sunny days,
his thoughts and actions wholly aimless,
oblivious of town and friend,
the functions he need not attend.

40

Our northern summer's a perversion
of winters further south of here;
it flickers briefly, a diversion
which fades as soon as it appears.
The sky was redolent of autumn,
the sun came into view but seldom,
the days had shortened steadily,
the woods' mysterious canopy,
despondent, murmured as it opened,
mist slowly settled on the leas,
a caravan of honking geese
was heading southwards like an omen;
a pallid season stood before –
November waited at the door.

41

A murky, icy dawn now rises,
the fields and meadows are now still,
a lurking hungry wolf surprises
the frightened horse which snorts and thrills,
the traveller is wary, nervous,
and sweeps uphill with jingling harness;
the herdsman, when the day begins,
now keeps his cows secure within,
so we no more can hear him calling
them with his horn back to the shed;
the maiden spins and bends her head
in her small hut, the wax is falling
from candles sending out their light,
those friends of deepest winter night.

42

The crackling hoarfrost soon imposes
itself on silver fields and trees,
(if you expect a rhyme with "roses",
go on then, I don't mind, feel free!),
the ice-clad waters shine and glimmer,
much more than polished floors can shimmer,
while noisily some skaters slice
their youthful way along the ice;
a heavy goose makes for the river
and plans a swim, laboriously
steps down and slithers clumsily,
with red feet flailing. Snow-flakes shiver –
the first glad flurries of the year –
and winter tells us it is here.

43

What can one do throughout this season?
Step out and stroll? The countryside's
an awful sight, and that by reason
of its inert, undignified
and naked state. Should one go riding
across the barren tundra, sliding
upon the treacherous ice below,
and risk a fall which lays you low?
Well, stay at home, however dreary,
and read de Pradt, or Walter Scott!
No fun? So tot up what you've got,
complain, or drink until you're cheery
again; the weeks will pass you by,
your winter woes will seem to fly.

44

Childe Harold–like, my friend Onegin
slipped into wistful lethargy;
an icy bath upon awaking,
he dressed, had breakfast and some tea,
then spent a while with calculations,
decided on some recreation,
blunt cue in hand, he thought he'd play
a game of billiards for the day,
and only stopped when it was evening.
Then balls and cue were left behind.
The table laid, he'd now unwind
before the fire, for Lenski's nearing,
conveyed by horses and a sleigh.
Come on, now, dinner's on the way!

45

Champagne is brought in for the poet,
that blessed, venerated wine,
some chilly Veuve Clicquot or Moët,
to buoy them up before they dine:
like Hippocrene it effervesces,
a simile, I must confess it,
reminding me of . . . various things!
It was my friend at countless flings,
I'd spend my last few measly coppers
on it – do you remember now
its captivating stream, and how
our manners verged on the improper,
the frequent jokes, the verses, rhymes,
the arguments, those dream-filled times?

46

But now its sparkling froth betrays me,
and I prefer demure Bordeaux:
its very staidness always saves me
from heartburn, leaving me aglow.
Champagne is like a brilliant mistress
who finds me far too dull and listless,
she's volatile and glittering,
yet tritely wayward, twittering.
But you, Bordeaux, are like a comrade
who will in times of pain and grief
provide me with profound relief,
a true and steady trusted soul mate,
you share our leisure, joy and woe:
Long live my trusty friend, Bordeaux!

47

The fire is out, the embers smoulder
till there is little left to stoke,
the grate is growing ever colder,
yet sometimes curling wisps of smoke
drift up the chimney, and the glasses
stand sparkling as the daylight passes,
and pipes are lit. (I'm always pleased
to chat, imbibe, and feel at ease,
a bowl of wine upon the table,
before a smoking, blazing log
between the hours of wolf and dog,
though why they're called that I'm not able
to tell you). Be that as it may,
let's hear now what the two friends say.

48

"So how're the neighbours? How's Tatiana?
And Olga? Are they doing fine?"
"Fill up my glass before I answer . . .
Oh, that's enough! Please, no more wine!
They're doing well and send best wishes . . .
The girls are simply gorgeous, dishes . . .
And Olga's shoulders, bosom, soul . . .
Let's go there soon, yes, on the whole
that's best, would be appreciated,
and then, my friend, you can decide
if I am not quite justified . . .
You've been there twice, they'd be elated . . .
Oh what a fool I am! Don't speak!
We've got to visit them next week!"

49

"What, *me*?" "Yes, you! It's Tanya's name day!
Olinka and her family
have asked us over, and there's *no* way
that you'll refuse both them and me!"
"But there will be so many people,
all sorts of riff-raff, old and feeble . . . "
"Come on, that's rubbish, just a joke!
There'll only be her closest folk!
Let's go! Say yes! Do me the favour!
O.K?" "All right, it seems I must . . . "
"I'm glad you've not betrayed my trust."
And drinking to his pretty neighbour,
he talked of Olga's charms anew
quite ceaselessly. That's love for you!

50

He was ecstatic: in a fortnight
his longed-for wedding would take place,
the marriage bed would be the highlight
of his young life; he could embrace
the mysteries of passion's transports,
not giving any anxious forethought
to Hymen's many woes and chores,
for wedlock is an awful bore!
But we, the enemies of Hymen,
we know the weary, tedious pains
of life at home, as Lafontaine
in sentimental tales described them.
Poor Lenski was, I fear, at heart
ordained to play that selfsame part.

51

He was adored – at least he thought so –
and thus was overjoyed and thrilled.
Contented he who's free of sorrow
and blest with faith, who's also stilled
his intellect to find true calmness,
untroubled like some drunkard, legless;
more aptly, like a butterfly
exploring flowers in July.
But sad the man who knows what's coming,
whose head has never been confused,
whom word and deed have not bemused –
perceiving all, he's always thumbing
his nose at everything, it seems,
and has no time to lose in dreams.

CHAPTER FIVE

Never know these frightful dreams,
my dear Svetlana!

Zhukovski

CHAPTER FIVE

1

That year the warm and autumn weather
appeared to wish that it could stay,
and nature dawdled, altogether
reluctant ever to make way
for winter; suddenly some flurries
of shining snow arrived and hurried
to cover fences, houses, lanes,
drew patterns on the window panes.
Tatiana wakes and sees the whitened
and gleaming countryside; the trees
in wintry silver, magpies please
her eyes, the hills around now lighten
as swirling snowflakes gently float,
enclosing all in winter's coat.

2

So now it's winter-time! The peasant
sets off, rejoicing in the day,
his horse, in snow both crisp and pleasant,
is snorting as it drags the sleigh,
while fleet kibitkas glide for hours
and throw up fluffy, snowy showers;
the coachman drives with proud panache
in sheepskin coat and crimson sash;
a country urchin blithely lingers
amidst the snow and pulls his sled
on which a mongrel sits, instead
of him; he laughs at frozen fingers,
inflamed in all the biting cold,
not caring as his mother scolds.

3

Perhaps you don't find this seductive,
such scenes of country life and deeds?
Well, lowly nature's not attractive,
quite unrefined, one must concede.
Another poet's inspiration
has painted charming evocations
of winter hues and falling snow
and all the beauty then on show;
I'm sure you'll find him edifying,
depicting sleighs on secret rides
in words sublime and rarefied;
but have no fear, for I'm not trying
to copy him nor, I'm afraid,
that bard who lauds his Finnish maid.

4

Tatiana (in her soul so Russian,
although she hardly realised why),
adored the Russian winter: frozen
enchantment in an icy sky,
the frosty sun on fields and hedges,
the rosy dawns, the speeding sledges,
the evenings at Epiphany.
The Larins, as a family,
observed the feast at home according
to custom; servant girls foretold
the fortunes of the ladies, bold
predictions which were most rewarding,
for every year they prophesied
that each would be a soldier's bride.

5

Tatiana thought that ancient folklore
assuredly was all too true,
so dreams and laying cards were therefore
like portents of the moon, a clue
to future happiness, forewarnings,
mysterious and often daunting;
small incidents of any kind
disturbed the quiet of her mind:
the pompous tomcat, purring, leering,
upon the stove might wash its face,
and this would cause her heart to race,
for guests undoubtedly were nearing;
or if she suddenly espied
the sickle moon on her left side,

6

she'd pale with dread and start to quiver;
or if a meteor should fall
and rush across the sky to shiver
as it broke up, she'd soon tell all
her secret wishes and her yearnings
to such a star while it was burning;
and should she ever chance to sight
a black-cowled monk, she'd freeze with fright;
a darting rabbit would engender
alarm if it should cross her trail,
anxiety would turn her pale –
such episodes would always render
her sorrowful and, with a sense
of apprehension, nervous, tense.

7

And yet however great her terror,
she found a source of bliss and cheer
(nor is this strange, for man has ever
inclined to feel both joy and fear).
It's Christmas-time! There's great elation,
the youngsters practise divination,
although they're far too young to care
about what fate might hold prepared,
for life still stretches out before them.
The old folk also look ahead,
though almost blind, and nearly dead,
their future past, their present boredom.
But then, who cares? Hope mollifies
both young and old with childish lies.

8

Expectantly now Tanya's gazing
upon the wax within the dish,
its wondrous patterns are amazing,
proclaiming each and every wish.
Out of the bowl brimful with water
the maids pull rings in any order,
first one, then more, and when *her* ring
turns up they all begin to sing
a favourite and time-honoured ditty:
'The peasants there are always rich,
with spades they dig up silver which
will bring them fame and wealth.' Yet pity
pervades this song; much nicer's that
about the charming little cat.

9

The sky is clear, the night is frosty;
sublime, divine, a choir of light
meanders peacefully and softly . . .
Tatiana, in a low-cut, slight,
revealing mantle holds a mirror
towards the glowing moon which shimmers
alone in its dull glass . . . But hark!
The snow is creaking . . . In the dark
a passer-by; the girl then rushes
along on tip-toe up to him,
her little voice, refined and trim,
more tender than a flute, then gushes:
"What is your name?" Instead of one
she knows, he answers: "Agafon!"

10

Tatiana's nurse had then suggested
that she should place a meal for two
within the bath-house, and requested
that Tanya cast some spells she knew.
But fear soon clutched at Tatiana,
and I – remembering Svetlana –
would also be afraid. Oh well . . .
We'll not cast spells with her, nor dwell
on that. Tatiana soon undresses
and goes to bed, as cupids waft
above her pillow, downy, soft,
on which she lays her flowing tresses;
beneath it lies the looking glass,
she sleeps in peace, the hours pass . . .

11

Tatiana's now asleep and dreaming:
she dreams that it's a snowy night,
she's walking on a plain in seeming
eternal gloom; she catches sight,
quite unexpected, of an urgent,
tumultuous and freezing torrent,
that winter still has left unchained,
which churns and tumbles unrestrained;
sees two thin poles, both stuck together
with ice, a wobbly, trembling bridge
across the raging waters, which
is where she stops and goes no further;
perplexed at first, she hesitates
and in that dreadful din, she waits.

12

As if she fears a doleful parting,
Tatiana grumbles at the stream;
She feels abandoned, puzzled, smarting,
that she can't cross, so it would seem,
for no one's near to give assistance.
But then a snowdrift in the distance
begins to move, and who is there?
A large and very shaggy bear!
Tatiana shrieks, the beast starts roaring,
then stretches out a hairy paw;
she nerves herself and holds a claw
on which she leans with care, exploring
her way across the brook to find
the bear is trotting on behind.

13

She hurries onwards, ever quicker,
and does not risk a backward glance;
her hairy escort's always with her,
she hasn't got the slightest chance
of shaking off her grunting vassal.
A wood appears. The trees are tranquil
in all their frowning elegance;
the weight of snow is quite immense
upon the branches; through the summits
of barren aspens, birches, limes,
the glow of dazzling night-time shines.
There is no pathway; bushes, moonlit
escarpments all lie deep below
great mounds of shifting, drifting snow . . .

14

The bear accompanies our Tanya
into the forest where the trees
and bushes suddenly attack her,
as snow engulfs her to the knees.
A twig tears out her golden earrings,
her small wet shoes are lost in searing,
benumbing snow; she then lets fall
her handkerchief, no time at all
to pick it up, she's spent and frightened,
can always hear the lumbering bear
behind her, and she doesn't dare
to raise her skirt so she might righten
its hem line as she flees; at length
she falls, for gone is all her strength.

15

She's lying in the snow – so, nimbly,
the bear scoops up the fainting girl
and carries her, scarce breathing, quickly
along a road; her senses whirl,
she hardly stirs; then, unexpected,
a humble hovel, all protected
by dense and murky woods, stands there
and on it snow lies everywhere,
while from a window light shines brightly;
within the hovel voices yell;
the bear remarks: "You'll soon feel well,
my friend lives here," he growls politely.
The brute then marches through the door
and lays the girl upon the floor.

16

Tatiana stirs, then looks around her:
the bear has gone, she's lying in
a hallway; wits and senses flounder
at all the mindless, ceaseless din.
As if it were some wake or party,
the guests are drinking, hale and hearty;
she hears the glasses as they clink,
so peering shyly through a chink
she sees – sees something quite perturbing:
a table at which monsters sit,
a dog-faced beast with horns, a witch
with goatee beard and, most disturbing,
a skeleton, a dwarf, a cock,
a cat-like bird complete the shock.

17

More frightful still, and more amazing,
a spider on which squats a crab,
a goose-necked skull on which is waving
a reddish cap; a windmill jabs
and grinds its swirling arms while dancing.
Loud barks and laughter, singing, prancing,
applause and whistling, ghastly sounds,
a stamping horse are what she found,
and yet what must she have been thinking
when unexpectedly she saw
a guest she loved and held in awe:
the hero of our tale is drinking
with all these creatures standing by,
while staring round with furtive eye.

18

He gives a sign – they start to scurry.
He takes a drink – they sip and squawk.
He laughs – they cackle in a hurry.
He knits his brows – and they don't talk.
Apparently he is their master!
Tatiana's heart now beats no faster,
and as she is quite curious
to see the cause of all the fuss,
she fiddles with the door, is startled
when howling winds blow out the light . . .
the gang of goblins quails with fright,
Onegin's eyes begin to sparkle
with rage; he pushes back his chair
and goes to see who's standing there.

19

Then suddenly she's gripped by panic
and quickly tries to get away.
Impossible! She's almost manic
with fear, and then she starts to sway;
she wants to scream, but isn't able . . .
Onegin rushes past the table,
he grabs the door and so displays
the girl to every monster's gaze.
Ferocious laughter breaks out wildly
and then the eyes of one and all
examine her; strange creatures bawl:
moustaches, trotters, tusks and slimy
proboscises, a finger-bone,
these phantoms cry: "She's mine alone!"

20

"Oh no, she's *mine*!" Onegin bellows
and straight away the company
departs; Tatiana in the shadows
remains alone with him and he
proceeds to pull her gently into
a corner; Tanya does not argue;
he sits her on a shaky chair
and lets his head sink on her hair
and shoulder. Olga enters quickly,
behind her Lenski; then a light
shines out, as Tanya catches sight
of Eugene staring wildly as he
harangues the guests and flails about.
Poor Tanya falls and passes out.

21

The uproar grows, becoming coarser,
when suddenly Onegin grabs
a knife; he lashes out with force and
directly someone falls; the drab
and dismal shadows seem to thicken.
A dreadful scream . . . poor Lenski's stricken . . .
The hovel shudders . . . Tanya wakes
in terror, stupefied, and takes
a look . . . The room is light already.
She sees the scarlet gleam of morn
through frosty windows, it is dawn . . .
Then in flits Olga, rosy, heady,
a flighty swallow, who then cheeps:
"And what did you see in your sleep?"

22

But Tanya, paying no attention,
continues reading in her bed,
she seemingly has no intention
of speaking, not a word is said,
for she's engrossed in an old treatise
containing neither lyric riches
nor learnéd truths, and plainly not
the work of Byron, Virgil, Scott . . .
Not even Seneca has ever
so gripped a girl, nor has Racine,
or any fashion magazine
as much as Martin Zadeck's clever
critique of dreams, whose every page
reveals the wisdom of a sage.

23

This weighty work a roving vendor
had brought to their secluded home;
Tatiana also thought she'd spend her
small funds on further dusty tomes:
Malvina, for three roubles fifty,
with which he also threw in swiftly
a grammar and some simple tales,
book three of Marmontel, some pale
and feeble verses on Tsar Peter.
As time went by the Zadeck was
her dearest confidant because
it told what destiny might bring her,
if joy or woe. She always kept
it near, awake and when she slept.

24

Tatiana finds her dream disturbing,
so she decides to have a look
if there's a prospect of unearthing
its deeper meaning in her book.
She searches through the little index
and finds among the list of contents
a bear, a fir, a footbridge, gloom,
a hedgehog, raven, snowstorm: doom
in every shape and size. Her problem
remains unsolved despite her search,
for Zadeck's left her in the lurch!
The threatening dream's a sad conundrum,
foretelling trouble, she is sure
which in the next days she'll endure.

25

And then the crimson hand of morning
together with the rising sun
leads forth a glorious dawn adorning
the festive name day, filled with fun.
The Larins' house begins quite early
to pulse with guests, and soon is fairly
jam-packed, whole families converge,
kibitkas, britskas, sledges surge
towards the house, the people jostle
in vestibule and drawing room
as laughter sounds and voices boom;
the noise and crush are quite colossal,
made even worse by barking pekes
and bawling nurses, babies' shrieks.

26

Fat Pustyakov with his stout lady,
Gvozdin, a landlord much admired,
whose serfs were destitute and mangy,
the Skotinins, grey-haired and tired,
with countless children of all ages,
from two-year olds to semi-sages;
and then there's footling Petushkóv
who's known to all, the local toff;
and here's my cousin, old Buyánov
(bedecked with fluff, and known to you);
now look who's just hove into view,
State Councillor (retired) Flyánov,
a scandalmonger, glutton, wretch,
who takes a bribe, a shocking lech!

27

Then Harlikov and all his household
appeared, and with them came a wit:
Monsieur Triquet now crossed the threshold,
bespectacled and literate,
accoutred in a wig, a Frenchman
who'd brought a verse (not his invention)
set to the children's melody
"Reveillez-vous, belle endormie"
for Tanya, which he'd found while searching
among some ancient almanacs
awash with rhymes by hoary hacks.
Triquet, then cleverly inserting
his own idea, changed "belle Niná"
into "la belle Ta-tí-a-ná".

28

The darling of the older ladies
and apple of each mother's eye,
a bigwig from the army bases,
arrives – brings news which gratifies
the company – the regimental
commander plans an instrumental
performance, it has been decreed:
"The general himself, indeed,
has ordered it!" he's heard announcing.
What joy! There's going to be a ball!
Delight suffuses one and all.
But dinner's served, the young girls flouncing,
the guests in pairs go in to dine,
to gorge themselves on meat and wine.

29

Then for a while the guests are silent,
they're busy chewing at their fare;
on every side there is the strident
commotion made by tableware
which rattles, while the clink of glasses
reveals that as the dinner passes
the guests are slowly coming round
and growing restive, festive, loud,
soon talking, laughing, squealing, shouting;
the door flies open suddenly
and Lenski enters, rapidly
Onegin follows. "How astounding!"
their hostess cries, "we're truly blest!"
The two friends join the other guests,

30

are seated side by side and facing
Tatiana, who has turned quite pale,
just like the morning moon that's waning,
as nervous as a hunted, frail
and timid fawn; her eyes grow darker,
she glances down, she's breathing faster
as passion glows tempestuously
within her; almost fainting, she's
quite near, it seems, to suffocation!
Indeed, she is so close to tears
that she completely fails to hear
the two friends' kindly salutation;
but reason and her strength of will
prevail; she answers, and keeps still.

31

Hysteria Onegin hated,
the girlish sobs and fainting fits
had left him feeling irritated,
for he had had his fill of it;
eccentric, maybe, yet the banquet
already had annoyed the hermit,
and now he found himself provoked
as Tanya all but wept and choked;
he looked away and started fuming,
he swore that he would soon avenge
himself on Lenski; his revenge
he saw before him, proudly looming . . .
and sketched a mental parody
of everyone that he could see.

32

Of course some others might have spotted
Tatiana's woes, had there not been
another object, choicely potted,
the finest pie they'd ever seen
(though oversalted rather badly);
then came a wine, a Tsimlyanski,
between the roast and the dessert
with glasses for it to be served,
those sparkling flutes, both tall and slender,
so like your trim and lissom waist,
and like my verse, Zizí, quite chaste,
you crystal jewel of your gender,
entrancing vial of my desire
which once I quaffed, obsessed, on fire.

33

Relieved of its now soggy stopper,
the bottle popped, the wine fizzed out.
Triquet stands up and, looking proper,
tormented by poetic doubt,
he sees before him watchful people;
Tatiana's feeling nervous, feeble,
awaiting things with mounting dread;
Monsieur Triquet now lifts his head,
begins to sing – it's not his forte,
he croaks, severely out of tune –
his little song; he's finished soon;
applause rings out, Tatiana curtsies,
the modest poet drinks and, worse,
presents her with his scrap of verse.

34

Congratulations are then offered,
Tatiana shows her gratitude;
it's now Onegin's turn to proffer
best wishes; Tanya's lassitude,
embarrassment, her anguished silence
aroused in him a sense of kindness,
he gave a deferential bow;
a tender look, he knew not how,
was in his eye. Perhaps he really
was touched or, being but a tease,
philandering with practised ease;
yet whether false or meant sincerely,
his friendly glance performed its part
in cheering Tanya's troubled heart.

35

The chairs, as they are shoved back, clatter,
the visitors now swarm into
the drawing room, their buzzing chatter
like bees in search of honeydew
who leave their quarters on their labours,
to seek out verdant meadows. Neighbours,
delighted with the feast, converse,
the girls are very soon immersed
in whispered gossip, while the matrons
content themselves beside the hearth;
then tables are set up for cards,
the older men play ombre, Boston,
there's whist for all, a trinity
of games born out of apathy.

36

Heroic rivals have completed
eight rubbers, seats have been exchanged
eight times: the players are next treated
to tea. (I'm happy to arrange
my life by lunch-time, tea, and supper;
we country people never suffer
from stress – our stomachs are our clocks);
and by the way, please don't be shocked
if I admit to you in passing
that I hold forth as frequently,
throughout this lengthy history,
on food as Homer; I'm not basking
in his renown, which we've revered
for something like three thousand years.

So – tea is served. The girls have hardly
got hold of cup and saucer, when
behind the ballroom doors abruptly
bassoon and flute resound and then,
delighted as the music carries,
friend Petushkóv, the local Paris,
goes up to Olga; Lenski asks
Tatiana if she'd like to dance;
Miss Harlikov, an ageing vestal,
is led out by Monsieur Triquet;
Bujánov, too, has joined the fray
with Pustyakov's good lady; festal
exuberance pervades the hall
in this most marvellous of balls.

40

When I began to write my story,
(compare, dear reader, chapter one),
I wished to picture all the glory
of balls in Petersburg, their fun
and splendour in Albano's fashion,
but was diverted by my passion
for ladies' slender feet I've known.
Enough's enough, for I have grown
fed up, oh little feet, of straying
upon your paltry meagre tracks;
at last it's time I turned my back
on all my misspent youth, betraying
myself no more, so chapter five
shall tell the truths for which I strive.

41

Monotonous and wholly crazy,
like youth's intense, frenetic whirl
the waltz's whirl is hazy, mazy,
as pair on pair gyrate and twirl.
The moment of revenge is nearing:
Onegin, smiling, almost sneering,
approaches Olga; rapidly
he dances with her, people see
him seat her in a chair, while talking
of this and that; but soon they start
again; they pirouette and dart
as they traverse the ballroom, waltzing
while everyone looks on amazed:
poor Lenski stares at them, quite dazed.

42

Musicians play, mazurkas thunder.
Time was, when music's deafening crash
could almost burst the floors asunder,
in ballrooms make the windows clash
and jar. Yet now all this has altered:
we're like the ladies, never falter,
and glide across the lacquered floor.
But in the country they are more
extreme, for there mazurka's kept its
unblemished charms: mustachios,
cavorting pairs on heels and toes
remain the same, are unaffected
by dictatorial, modish fads
which drive the modern Russian mad.

43/44

Buyánov, my intrepid cousin,
has taken both the sisters to
our hero; skilfully Onegin
has navigated Olga through
the dancers, gliding nonchalantly
and, bending over, elegantly
he breathes into her ear a verse,
some compliment, which promptly stirs
delight in Olga's haughty features,
as Eugene gives her hand a squeeze
she blushes and is clearly pleased;
my Lenski's seen it, almost speechless,
enraged, perplexed, he thereupon
asks Olga for the *cotillon*.

45

But no, she cannot! What's the matter?
She's promised Eugene the next dance!
Impossible! Good God! He's shattered!
Aghast, he's almost in a trance . . .
has heard . . . She could . . . how could that happen?
She's scarcely out of swaddling linen!
A child, a giddy child, and yet
well versed in cunning, a coquette
already expert in deception.
Poor Lenski does not have the strength,
he curses women at some length,
then leaves the glittering reception:
Two pistols, and we'll fix a date
to settle quickly both our fates.

CHAPTER SIX

Là, sotto i giorni nubilosi e brevi,
Nasce una gente a cui 'l morir non dole.
                                    Petrarch

CHAPTER SIX

1

On noticing that Lenski's vanished,
Eugene is soon fed up again,
his spirits then begin to languish,
though gratified by all the pain
he's caused his friend; then Olga, yawning,
reveals that she, too, finds it boring,
while seeking Lenski with her eyes;
the endless *cotillon* now tries
her patience, like some cruel vision;
but then it ends, it's supper-time,
and after that a bed's assigned
to every guest, a long procession
extending through the house, packed tight:
Eugene's gone home to spend the night.

2

Now all is quiet. In the parlour
the snores of Pustyakov resound;
exhausted by the splendid gala,
his better half snores just as loud,
while in the dining-room are seated,
asleep as well, their day completed,
Gvozdin, Buyánov, Pétushkóv,
and (feeling poorly) Flyanov,
there on the floor in underclothing
Monsieur Triquet has found his rest;
the girls are, one and all, the guests
of Olga, Tanya, where they're dozing:
illuminated by the moon,
Tatiana gazes from the room.

3

Onegin's unforeseen appearance,
his covert, fleeting, tender look,
his singular and constant nearness
to little Olga, all that shook
Tatiana to her soul, unable
to understand; a strangely painful
distrust descends, as if a cold
and icy hand had taken hold
of her and squeezed her heart, as if a
ravine had opened up and roared
beneath her . . . "Die, I'll die! but more
I cannot wish for!" Tanya whispers,
"To die for *him* is to be blest,
he'll never bring me happiness."

4

But forward! Forward, oh my story!
It's time to bring on a new face.
Five versts at most from Krasnogorie,
our Lenski's charming country place,
there lived and flourished quite serenely
in solitude the once unseemly
Zarétski, leader of a mob
of gamers, rogue and ale-house yob,
but now a bachelor and father
of sons and daughters, and a friend
on whom one really could depend,
magnanimous and also rather
a model of integrity:
how true a change of heart can be!

5

There'd been a time when fawning faces
had praised him for his pluck and nerve;
a splendid shot, at twenty paces,
he'd hit an ace with dashing verve.
By battle quite intoxicated,
his valour had been vindicated:
he'd tumbled from his Kalmuk steed,
while charging onward at great speed,
and landed in the mud, quite blotto!
The French looked on, incredulous,
and captured our new Regulus,
permitting the upstanding hero
to spend renewed captivity
imbibing wine unceasingly.

6

He'd always loved a laugh, however,
rejoiced in making fun of fools,
still more he liked to fool the clever,
their anger really made him drool,
although he, too, at times fell victim
to men who all too gladly tricked him,
while others wanted to repay
him for some nasty prank he'd played.
He was an expert at discussion,
knew when to be both quick and slow,
and when to keep his profile low,
how craftily to cause commotion,
make bitter foes of erstwhile friends,
who longed to duel in the end,

7

effect a reconciliation,
then take the pair of them to dine,
when with some witty exclamation
he'd slander them, jocose, malign . . .
Sed alia tempora! Young devils
(like lovers' dreams, and nightly revels)
relax when they begin to age;
Zarétski thus no longer raged
and fought, but in his pleasant bowers
of cherry trees, acacias,
sought refuge in Arcadia:
a sage, like Horace, growing flowers
while breeding birds, he found delight
in teaching kids to read and write.

8

He was not stupid. My Onegin
disliked Zarétski's sordid heart,
yet found his common sense engaging,
his acumen both brisk and smart.
Eugene was always pleased at seeing
Zarétski, so a morning meeting
did not surprise him; they exchanged
regards, their conversation ranged
around diverse affairs; abruptly,
a roguish twinkle in his eyes,
he gave Eugene, to his surprise,
a folded note for his eyes only
from Lenski, which Onegin read
alone, and not a word was said.

9

It was polite, "Your most obedient
and humble servant," Lenski said,
and challenged him, "when quite convenient",
to fight a duel, Eugene read.
Onegin turned round to Zarétski
and answered, slow and circumspectly,
that he was "ready any time."
Zarétski rose, said that was fine
and, not awaiting explanations,
decided he could stay no more,
for there were many different chores
to face; a sense of consternation
imbued Eugene, who stayed alone,
consumed by dark thoughts of his own.

10

It served him right, for when he questioned
his own behaviour secretly,
he keenly felt his indiscretion,
regretting he'd so casually
derided tender, timid passion
the night before in such a fashion;
and, furthermore, a poet may
behave in such a foolish way,
particularly when the fellow
is but eighteen! Eugene adored
the youthful poet, and he ought
to have resisted all such shallow
stupidities, and proved to be
a man of sense and decency.

11

He should have shown some friendly feeling
and not have bridled like a beast,
sought out a tactful way of healing
hostility and hurt, at least.
"But it's too late, for now that cruel
old man is party to the duel,"
he muses, "smooth and mouthy, bad . . . ,
although good sense might keep the cad
from gossiping and making wisecracks,
and yet the whispers of the fools
would open me to ridicule . . ."
Publicity has certain drawbacks,
although we never find it odd
that we make pride and fame our God!

12

With constantly decreasing patience
our poet waits at home for news . . .
His high-flown neighbour makes his entrance
and brings an answer to the youth.
The jealous suitor swells with pleasure,
he'd been afraid that in some measure
Eugene would treat it as a hoax,
avoid the threat by cracking jokes,
inventing methods of escaping
the pistol pointed at his breast;
these fears had now been laid to rest . . .
Tomorrow morning after waking
they'd meet to aim at thigh or head
and try to shoot each other dead.

13

Resolved that he would hate his rival,
the poet did not wish to see
his Olga just before the duel,
he watched the clock uneasily,
but finally capitulating,
he found himself at Larins', waiting;
he feared he might upset the girl
and set her senses all awhirl,
but happily things were as ever.
As always, Olga tripped on down:
her merriment soon smoothed the frown
on Lenski's brow, her cheerful laughter,
untroubled, effervescent, gay,
just as on every other day.

14

"Why did you leave the house so early
last night?" Olinka promptly asked.
Confused, his thoughts still somewhat blurry,
the tongue-tied lover looked downcast;
annoyance, jealousy soon vanished,
in less than no time they were banished
before her limpid, guiltless gaze,
before her gentle, simple ways,
before her playful, lively spirit! . . .
He looked at her so tenderly,
and saw she loved him utterly,
remorse was gnawing at the poet,
perplexed, he looked for words in vain,
felt almost happy once again.

Yet suddenly he felt dejected,
reflective as he saw the lass,
so pretty that he soon rejected
all talk of yesterday as crass.
He thinks, "I'll be her worthy saviour,
won't brook such dissolute behaviour,
beguiling maiden hearts with lies,
false compliments and bogus sighs,
nor let the worthless, deadly serpent
devour the lily's tender shoots
or tear the youthful flower's roots,
scarce grown, and now no longer fragrant . . ."
And this all meant, my friends, you see:
I'll fight a comrade presently.

18

Had Lenski seen the awful anguish
that burned within my Tanya's soul,
had brooding Tanya not so languished,
if she had understood the whole
affair, that Lenski and Onegin
would in a little while be facing
each other in a fateful fight
for refuge in the tomb's dark night,
then possibly her pure devotion
might yet have reconciled the friends . . .
But no one noticed. In the end
Eugene stayed silent; raw emotion
left Tanya sad; the nurse alone,
had she been brighter, might have known.

19

All evening Lenski was distracted,
first reticent, then bold once more;
but those the muses have attracted
are thus; before the clavichord
he sat, with furrowed brow, now playing
a chord or two, his gaze then straying
to Olga, when he'd swiftly say,
"I'm happy, aren't I?" . . . He can't stay,
it's late . . . His laden heart was broken
and tightened as he took his leave
of his young love, and as he grieved
his inner self well-nigh burst open.
"All right?" she nervously enquired.
"I'm fine!" He hurriedly retired.

20

Arriving home, he first inspected
his pistols, which he then returned
to their old case, undressed, selected
some Schiller, though one prospect burned
within him: gloomy trepidation
ruled out all thought of relaxation.
His Olga's lovely form and face
appeared to him in all their grace:
the poet slowly shut the volume,
picked up his pen and wrote some verse –
jam-packed with tosh, to make things worse,
with love's clichés and sickly perfume –
ecstatically he read it through,
like drunken Delvig at a do!

21

This work, by chance, has been safeguarded,
I have it still, so here it is:
"Oh where, Oh where have you departed,
my springtime's golden days of bliss?
What lies in store for me tomorrow?
In vain I've tried to see the sorrow
awaiting me and hidden deep
beyond the murky mists of sleep.
It matters not, for fate's fair-minded:
should I be pierced by its sharp dart,
or should it miss my aching heart,
it's just! I'll take it as I find it.
Blest be the day with all its grief,
blest too the night, which brings relief.

22

"When night-time's passed and day is dawning,
the sun begins to scintillate,
perhaps I'll sink into the yawning
protection of the tomb and wait
till Lethe swamps the poet's callow
remembrance, and the world, so shallow,
ignores me; still, my fairest maid,
you'll not forget me, I won't fade
for you; you'll shed a tear in honour
of me upon my urn, and say:
'To me belonged the early days
of this unhappy life! My lover,
my friend, oh hoped-for spouse of mine,
oh come, oh come, for I am thine!' "

23

That's how he wrote, 'obscurely', 'limply'
('Romanticism', I believe,
though what's romantic here I simply
am quite unable to perceive!
But then, who cares?) As dawn approaches,
his head sinks lower and he dozes,
just at the modish word "Ideal",
when hopes of sleep at last seem real.
No sooner has he started napping
than suddenly his neighbour comes;
he wakes poor Lenski, still benumbed
and silent in his study, tapping
his arm, "Come on, it's time to go!
Onegin's waiting in the snow."

24

But he was wrong! Eugene is lying
unconscious in his feather bed.
The shadows of the night are dying,
the morning star gleams overhead,
saluted by the cockerel crowing
the sun has risen, snow is blowing
in sparkling turmoil through the air;
Eugene's asleep, quite unaware
of all the world around him; slowly
awaking, daylight permeates
the bedchamber; he hesitates,
then draws apart the curtains fully
and sees the glowing light of day:
it's time that he was on his way!

25

He rings the bell. The valet scurries
(Guillot, a Frenchman), brings his shoes,
his clothes and robe; Onegin hurries
to dress, he knows there's much to do.
Guillot is ordered not to tarry,
but drive the sledge and also carry
the pistol-case along with him.
A racing-sleigh is there to skim
across the snow; Eugene climbs onto
the seat and steels himself to fly
towards the mill; they soon draw nigh,
he bids his servant check the venue,
then fetch the guns, remove his cloak
and stand the horses by an oak.

26

Impatient from the lengthy waiting,
the poet leans upon the sluice;
Zarétski's confidently slating
the millstone, claiming it's no use!
Eugene appears, apologises . . .
"But where's," Zarétski agonises,
"your second?" Concerning duelling,
he was a pedant. All such things
must be precisely regulated,
a man could simply not be killed!
The proper code must be fulfilled,
as custom has so long dictated,
conforming to the wonted ways,
(for which he merits every praise!)

"My second?" answered Eugene keenly,
"He's here, Monsieur Guillot, my friend.
I can't see anything unseemly
in that, I'm happy to depend
on him. He might be unimportant,
but he is honest, has deportment."
Zarétski bit his lip, upset.
Eugene enquired, "You ready yet?"
"If you are, so am I!" said Lenski
and both of them moved to the mill,
while at a distance, pensive, still,
the 'honest friend' and old Zarétski
began in detail to liaise:
the foes both sank their nervous gaze.

The foes! Has ancient bloodlust severed
their friendship? Don't they both recall
that they had shared their past together,
their thoughts, their meals, their lives, their all?
And now, as if in some vendetta
whose nightmare wraiths they couldn't fetter,
irrational, mysterious,
the rivals waited, dangerous,
and bent on their annihilation . . .
Should they not both grin sheepishly,
and part as friends, unblemished, free?
Recall their love and admiration?
And yet the *beau monde* loves to hate:
remorse is thus the worst of fates.

29

The pistols gleam, the priming hammer
resounds against the ramrod head;
the bullets drop, pushed by the rammer,
the lever clicks, the powder's fed
in little greyish streams to trickle
into the pan; the rough and brittle,
securely fastened flint is raised
again. Guillot stands, wholly dazed,
behind a nearby tree stump; meanwhile,
their cloaks removed, they're face to face . . .
Zarétski has exactly paced
the thirty-two steps, quick and agile,
he shows the rivals where to stand,
each with a pistol in his hand.

30

"Commence at will!" So walking coldly,
not aiming yet, the two men move
towards each other, striding boldly,
four steps, four fatal steps they prove . . .
Eugene, not pausing for a moment,
advances nearer his opponent
and is the first to raise his arm.
Then five more steps with lethal calm
and Lenski, trembling arm extended,
has closed his left eye. Suddenly
Onegin fires and instantly
the stroke of fate has now descended . . .
In awful silence Lenski stops
and then his pistol slowly drops . . .

31

His hands explore his breast an instant . . .
Then he too falls, his clouded gaze
is that of death, not pain, quite vacant,
just as on certain sunlit days
a sparkling wedge of snow will tumble
unhurriedly downhill, he stumbles . . .
Engulfed in sudden freezing fear,
Onegin darts along to peer
at Lenski, calls his name, but vainly:
the poet's gone, an unkind fate
has dealt its blow, it's now too late,
the icy storm has passed. Profanely
at sunrise death dries out the bloom,
the altar candle's plunged in gloom.

32

Inert he lay, a strange and pallid
serenity upon his brow;
right through his chest the deadly bullet
had passed; the steaming blood flowed now
where moments earlier inspiration,
aversion, love and expectation
had throbbed, where blood had boiled and seethed,
where life had shimmered, spirit breathed;
but here, as in a house, unlightened
and bare, where all is empty, chill,
this heart remains forever still,
the shutters closed, the windows whitened
with chalk. The chatelaine has left,
all traces gone, the place bereft.

33

It's fun to watch one's rival bumbling,
annoy him with a cheeky quip;
it's fun to see him coarsely humbling
himself: with thrusting horns he trips
and staggers, glimpsing in the mirror
unwittingly with sudden terror
and odium his silly face;
yet nicer still when he's not braced
to grasp the truth, and starts to bellow:
"It's me!" More entertaining yet
to dig a grave for him, not fret,
then shoot him through the head, poor fellow.
Well, that's what *I* so like to do,
though maybe that's not true of *you*!

34

But what if you've just terminated
the life of a devoted friend,
whose saucy glances, calculated
bon mots or bagatelles offend
you deeply while you're blithely drinking,
who's even challenged you, unthinking,
annoyed? How would you grieve and feel,
would not your wretched spirit reel,
as he lies lifeless and unmoving
before you on the ground, with death
upon his ashen brow, his breath
now still, glazed stare reproving,
struck dumb, quite deaf to every plea,
how broken-hearted would you be?

35

Despairing, filled with harsh contrition,
the pistol dangling in his hand,
he looks at Lenski, premonition
upon his face; his neighbour, bland,
remarks, "Well, well, he's dead!" Onegin's
appalled: he calls his men, heart racing,
and walks away. Zarétski lays
the frozen body on the sleigh
and drives the hideous consignment
from thence: the horses shy and snort,
they smell the corpse and, quite distraught,
react by plunging with excitement,
and champing at the bit, they foam,
bewildered, as they speed for home.

36

My friends! You're sorry for the poet
just on the threshold of success:
before he's had the time to show it,
scarce out of childish ways and dress,
he's been laid low, the bloom has faded,
all passion's gone, ambition jaded,
exalted tender fearless thoughts
and sentiments all brought to naught . . .
now where are love's tempestuous longings,
the thirst for knowledge and for toil,
the fear of shame and vice, which spoil
it all, and where the musings, thronging
imaginings of mystery,
of dreams and sacred poetry?

37

Ordained perhaps for worldly grandeur,
maybe to do mankind some good,
his silenced lyre has lost its splendour . . .
In centuries to come it could
have yielded music, vibrant, fearless,
the poet might have climbed to peerless,
undreamed of heights awaiting him;
his murdered, martyred shadow, dim
and gloomy, might perhaps have taken
some consecrated mystery
along with it; we've lost a free
and ardent voice; entombed, forsaken,
it now lies far beyond acclaim:
the nations will not bless his name.

38/39

But then again, it's not unlikely
the poet might have faced the fate
of most of us: no longer sprightly,
the days of youth evaporate,
the soul abates in its endeavours,
in many ways you've changed forever.
First married, then, the muse betrayed,
provincial life, cuckolded, staid,
until a jacket, warm and quilted,
is all that's left! At last you see,
aged forty plus, reality,
have feasted, sulked, got fat, then wilted
and, ringed by weeping brood and wife,
while doctors watch, depart this life.

40

But be that as it may, dear reader,
our poet's life is at an end;
the youthful lover, pensive dreamer
alas, shot dead by his good friend.
There is a place quite near the village
where this dear child of verse and knowledge
had dwelt: two pines have intertwined,
nearby some snaking brooklets wind,
becoming swirling, tumbling rivers
in valleys where the ploughman rests,
the harvest maidens pass and jest
when they replenish ringing pitchers;
and by a brook in deepest shade
a simple shrine stands in a glade.

41

Beneath it (when the year is waiting
to bless the fields with rain in spring)
the herdsman sits there, deftly braiding
his mottled shoes of bast, and sings
of Volga fishermen; in summer
a city lady, a newcomer,
will ride through pastures on her own
and suddenly espy the stone:
she'll halt her steed, and then she'll tighten
the leather reins, while bending down
turn up her veil, adjust her gown,
and contemplate the shrine; enlightened,
the simple text will make her sigh
as she attempts to dry her eye.

42

And riding over endless meadows
she'll sink into a reverie,
reflect on Lenski, the poor fellow,
his fate, and on the destiny
of Olga: "Did she feel great sorrow,
or weep today and laugh tomorrow?
And where's her sister now, and where's
that man of modish, voguish airs
who tilts at modish, voguish beauties,
who slew the poet that sad day,
then fled the world and all its ways,
eccentric, with no sense of duty?"
I'll tell you everything perforce,
each smallest detail in due course,

43

but not quite yet! Although I treasure
my hero still with all my heart
and will return to him with pleasure,
the time has come for us to part.
The years incline towards a season
of solemn prose, I see no reason
to chase the playful maid of rhyme
and I no longer have the time
or wish – and sighing, I'll concede it,
I slowly follow on behind;
my pen has lost the will to grind
out vapid verses: now I need it
for other, colder, sterner themes
disturbing both my days and dreams.

44

I've heard the voice of different yearnings,
I've known a new despondency;
the first are fruitless, I'm now learning,
while bygone sorrows sadden me.
My dreams, my dreams of sun and roses,
now where (slick rhyme!) are youth's smart poses?
Can it be true that suddenly
my laurel wreath's gone finally?
Be true beyond all reservation –
all elegiac wiles aside –
that my life's springtime in its pride
(as I have joked without cessation)
is gone for good? If I'm not wrong,
I'm thirty soon – it won't be long!

45

And so my noontide has just started,
I must accept it, that I see,
so let's stay friends now we have parted,
oh youth, which I've spent carelessly.
My thanks for all the hours of gladness,
the torments and the cherished sadness,
for all the storms, the feasts and pranks,
for all your bounty, take my thanks:
in all of them I have delighted
amidst the quiet and the noise,
for everything, the woes and joys,
my gratitude. Enough! Excited,
untroubled, free from every strife,
I'll try to rest from my old life.

46

So I'll glance back. Farewell, you hidden
and silent groves in which I spent
my fleeting days, in which unbidden
both sloth and passion came and went;
and you, my youthful inspiration,
stir up my blithe imagination,
refresh my torpid, dormant soul
and make my lone retreat your goal,
let not my poet's heart sense coolness,
grow weary, calloused, dry as bone
until it hardens into stone
amongst the world's befuddled crudeness,
this mire in which, dear friends, we're swathed,
this swamp in which the whole world's bathed.

CHAPTER SEVEN

Moscow! Russia's favourite daughter!
Where is your equal to be found?
                                Dmitriev

How can one not love one's native Moscow?
                                Baratïnski

"Attacking Moscow! This is what comes from seeing the world!
Where is it better, then?"
"Where we are not."

                                Griboedov

CHAPTER SEVEN

1

Pursued by springtime's warming sunshine,
the snow is chased from off the hills
and runs in swelling streams through alpine
escarpments where it swirls and spills
on inundated fields and meadows.
Now tranquil Nature, sleepy, mellow,
salutes the morning of the year;
the heavens glisten, blue and clear,
the yet translucent trees are growing
unhurriedly, a downy green,
the bees amidst the flowers glean
their tribute while the herds are lowing;
the earth grows dry and nightingales
delight the silent, moonlit vales.

2

How sad my spirit at your coming,
o Spring, love's season, blissful Spring!
What throbbing agitation, flooding
both turbid blood and soul, you bring!
With what a tender, drowsy feeling
I bask in spring's sweet fragrance, reeling,
as in the lap of rural calm
it fans my face with glowing balm!
Or is all happiness a stranger,
is everything that gladdened me,
all radiance and ecstasy,
now dull and wearisome, a danger
to soul and spirit long since dead,
which darkens all it sees with dread?

3

When winter's past, do we remember
some bitter loss, not overjoyed
that leaves which mouldered last November
are here again? Are we annoyed,
as breezes whisper through the woodlands,
at our so transient existence
to which we never can return,
unlike the spring for which we yearn?
Perhaps while we are lost in musing
on loveliness, the thought might come
into our brooding mind of some
departed, former spring, suffusing
our hearts with dreams of distant climes,
of moonlit nights and wondrous times . . .

4

Now is the day! Good sluggards, loungers,
wise Epicureans, lazy fools,
indulged and pampered playboys, scroungers,
young poets of Lyóvshin's school,
you rustic Priams, sentimental
idealistic girls, the gentle,
alluring voice of springtime calls
you to the country, one and all,
the season bright with warmth and flowers,
with work and merry, festive strolls,
seductive nights for ardent souls . . .
My friends, be quick! Within the hour
hitch up a horse and fill your cart,
the meadows wait, so make a start!

5

And you, dear reader, leave the city
where you have spent the winter months
with dancing, laughter, being witty;
procure a carriage, go at once
to join my wilful muse's humour
and hear the parks and meadows murmur
above some nameless gurgling brook,
where my Eugene once undertook
his lonely hermit's life, both slothful
and wretched in the winter days,
with Tanya not so far away,
my lovely dreamer, pensive, soulful –
although he's now no longer there,
no vestige of him anywhere . . .

6

So let us go to where a crescent
of hills surrounds a tumbling burn
which winds its way past rolling, pleasant
and verdant leas from whence it turns
and flows through lime-trees to a river.
The nightingale sets all aquiver,
Spring's lover sings the whole night through,
the wild rose blooms amidst the dew,
a fountain's heard, and in the distance
a simple weathered tombstone stands
beneath two ancient pine trees, and
upon it: "Here in Lonely Silence
Vladimir Lenski, Poet, Rests
in Peace among the Happy Blest."

7

There was a time when in the morning
the breezes played about a wreath
which strangely dangled there, adorning
a branch which veiled the urn beneath;
time was two girls on lazy evenings
appeared by moonlight, gently weeping,
embraced above the lonely tomb . . .
Today . . . The simple shrine is doomed
to be forgotten and neglected,
the path to it is weed-filled now,
no garlands dangle from the bough,
the herdsman, pallid and dejected,
will rest there, mend his shoe, and soon
begin to sing a wistful tune.

[8–9]
10

My poor old Lenski! Olga languished,
but not, it must be said, for long.
Alas! The young girl's awful anguish
proved fiery, if not very strong.
Another soon caught her attention,
with flattery made his intention
quite clear, and drove away the grief;
an uhlan's courtship brought relief
and now she is quite captivated:
an uhlan whom she finds a dear,
and lo! within the selfsame year
the girl's demurely celebrated
her wedding, happy, eyes ablaze,
while on her lips a light smile plays.

11

My poor old Lenski! Was the wretched
ill-fated poet terribly
distraught within his grave, secluded
in death by cold eternity,
at Olga's faithlessness? Or was he,
asleep and hushed with gentle balmy
oblivion, quite unperturbed,
on Lethe's waters undisturbed,
the world to him now closed and silent . . . ?
Yes! Total, absolute neglect
is all that we can dare expect
in death; companions in an instant
are hushed, and all we get to hear
is squabbling heirs, who scoff and sneer.

12

So Olga's ringing, merry laughter
was heard no more around the house;
the uhlan very soon thereafter
rejoined his regiment. His spouse
went with him, and her ageing mother
wept bitter tears she couldn't smother,
seemed scarce alive as her dear girl
departed in a frenzied whirl.
But Tanya didn't weep, a pallor
just spread across her doleful face,
so when the time came she was braced.
As they set off she showed great valour
and gamely waved to groom and bride,
remaining calm and dignified.

13

She watched the coach, as if surrounded
by some dense mist, and bravely stared,
for all her woes had been compounded.
She's now alone and in despair.
Alas! Her childhood's faithful comrade,
her loving bosom-friend and playmate
is gone, to her profound dismay,
ensnared by fate and swept away
for ever. Roaming like a shadow,
she wanders sadly, aimlessly,
and scans the garden . . . fruitlessly,
for all she finds is empty sorrow,
not joy nor ease for pent-up fears
but broken-hearted lonely tears.

14

And in her dreadful isolation
her passion burns, although unseen.
To aggravate her desolation
her heart reflects upon Eugene,
now far away. She wasn't willing
to pardon him for coldly killing
her brother, dead and buried, quite
forgotten; hardly out of sight,
his promised bride had found another.
All trace of him has long swept by
like smoke across an azure sky.
Perhaps there are two hearts which suffer
on his account – but I don't see
the point of all this misery.

15

Now it was evening and the darkness
came down, the waters calmly flowed,
as insects droned . . . A jolly chorus
of peasants ambled down the road,
while fishermen across the river
stoked smoking fires . . . the moonlight shimmered
upon the spacious, rolling leas,
as Tanya, sunk in reveries,
meandered lonely, never ceasing . . .
When unexpectedly she saw
a house with gracious grounds before
her, groves, a stream, a village, pleasing
and undisturbed. She stares, her heart
beats faster and begins to smart.

16

But in a moment doubts assail her:
"Should I go on? Should I turn round,
for he's not there?" Her courage fails her.
"I'll not intrude, just view the grounds,
the house, and then I'll go." She wanders,
scarce breathing, heart-in-mouth, then ponders,
confused, and ventures on into
the empty courtyard; dogs pursue
her, barking. At her exclamation
of fear a crowd of boys careers
towards her noisily and peers
around, then without hesitation
begins to separate the curs,
while carefully safeguarding her.

17

"I wonder, might one be permitted
to see the Master's house?" she asked.
Without delay the children flitted
away to fetch the key. At last
the maid Anisya came as briskly
as possible; the door was quickly
unlocked, and Tanya shyly stepped
into the house Onegin kept,
but vacant now. There in the parlour
a cue lay on the table top
and on the couch a riding crop.
Tatiana and the maid went farther:
"And here's the hearth," announced the crone,
"where once the Master sat alone.

18

"Our neighbour dined here in the evening
in winter, Lenski, who's now dead.
But follow me, we must be leaving . . .
Now here's the Master's den, his bed,
where he would spend his mornings reading
and take his coffee, hold a meeting
when his factotum would appear . . .
The former Master too lived here,
he'd put his specs on every Sunday
and by the window placidly
enjoy a game of cards with me.
May God's great love and mercy always
protect his precious bones and save
his spirit in his cold, damp grave."

19

Tatiana looks about with melting
and tender eyes at what she sees;
she finds the prospect overwhelming,
her mood improves immediately,
though not unmixed with painful pleasure . . .
She looks at all the simple treasures,
the darkened lamp, the piles of books,
the writing desk and, in a nook
beside the window covered by a
substantial rug, Onegin's bed.
In shadows which the moonlight sheds,
Lord Byron's portrait; somewhat higher
a louring bust upon a stand
with bicorn, folded arms and hands.

20

As if bewitched, Tatiana glances
around the modish hermit's cell
and is content. A chill wind dances
across the dale, a rocky fell
obscures the rising moon, mist shivers,
enclosing sleeping groves and rivers.
But it is late, high time to make
for home. Our youthful pilgrim takes
her leave; she gravely sighs, concealing
her agitation, and prepares
to start her journey back. She dares
to ask if no one minds her stealing
another chance quite soon to look
about the house and read the books.

21

When they had both walked past the gateway
she parted from the maid, and then,
arising early on the next day,
she went to see the house again
and, entering the silent study
forgot the world and everybody.
Secluded now, and desolate,
increasingly disconsolate,
she wept, then started to examine
the books, at first without concern,
but in a while she had discerned
that some seemed strange, so she determined
to have a look, was soon engaged
in reading, and her world was changed!

22

Although we know that books no longer
amused Eugene, a few of them
had been exempted from dishonour!
The bard who hadn't been condemned
was he of Don Juan, the Giaour
and two or three choice novels, flowers
grown of the age, reflecting it
and modern Man (immoderate,
licentious, selfish, always scheming,
who, listless, filled with self-esteem,
is fond of dissipated dreams),
portrayed here accurately, teeming
with dry and bitter, churlish thoughts,
his way of life absurdly fraught.

23

On many sides she recognises
the trenchant marks of fingernails;
attentively she scrutinises
those sections, seeing without fail,
which passages and observations
had found Onegin's admiration,
with which he'd tacitly agreed,
where in the ample margins he'd
impatiently once pencilled in some
remark or underlined a phrase;
each one of them in various ways
revealed Onegin's soul. No system,
a brief word here, an asterisk,
a question mark, impulsive, brisk.

24

And so my Tanya starts quite slowly
to understand beyond all doubt –
thank God – the one whom fate had solely
ordained for her to dream about
and sigh for. Creature out of heaven
or hell? Dejected, freakish demon?
Is he an angel or a fiend,
benign, or brutally demeaned?
Who is he then? An imitation?
A paltry vision or some joke,
a Muscovite in Harold's cloak?
A lexicon of strange creations,
a rare and modish glossary?
Could he not be a parody?

25

So has she solved the vexing riddle?
And has she found the proper 'word'?
The time flies by, and in the middle
of her reflections she's disturbed
by thoughts of home, where she's awaited
to meet two neighbours who'll be feted
with tea; their conversation dwells
upon her, as her mother tells
the guests her woes: "I am so worried,
Tatiana is now fully grown,
Olinka has already flown
the nest some time ago. She's married,
but Tanya will not find a man,
she mopes in forests when she can."

26

"Perhaps she is in love?" "With whom then?
Buyánov offered, she refused.
With Pétushkov she was so stubborn,
Hussar Pikhtin was so bemused
by Tanya, he's cajoled and kept her
amused, I felt he would accept her,
but should have known, for nothing came
of it!" "Dear lady, what a shame!
So tell me now, what is the problem?
To Moscow, that's where you should go,
as it's the place for brides, you know."
"But, my dear Sir, the cost is fearsome!"
"You've money for one winter, come!
And if you're short, I'll lend you some."

27

This kind advice much pleased the mother,
she found it sensible and good.
She paused a moment – then another –
and then decided that she would
set out for Moscow in the winter,
and Tanya hears the awful rumour . . .
To let the mocking gossips see
her rural, clear simplicity,
her dated clothes and dated language,
be stared at by some Moscow toff
or shameless sirens showing off,
be laughed at like some rustic savage!
No, no! Much better she should stay
in her small world, and far away!

28

She rises as the day is dawning
and wanders with the sunshine through
the fields, and feasts her eyes all morning
on them, aglow with sparkling dew.
"Farewell," she murmurs, "peaceful valley,
you hilltops where I loved to dally,
and you, familiar woods and groves
through which we often strolled and drove,
farewell, serene, celestial beauty,
farewell, you blissful scenery,
forsaken now for vanity,
farewell, my freedom, it's my duty.
Oh what and where will be my fate?
For what and wherefore must I wait?"

29

Her walks continue, ever longer,
a hillock here, or there a brook;
she visits them, the pull grows stronger
and forces her to stop and look,
as they enchant her with their calming
allure, like well-loved friends, disarming
and kind, she runs to see and talk
to woods and fields through which she walks.
The fleeting summer passes quickly,
the golden autumn's here again,
and Nature, tremulous and faint,
is like some victim decked out richly . . .
Then driving, howling from the North,
the winter sorceress stepped forth.

30

She came and cast her spell around her
and hung in clusters from the trees,
reclined in rippling layers, found her
abode amidst the hills and leas;
the frozen brook and the embankment
lay softly covered, silent, dormant,
frost gleamed; how fine her sleights of hand,
delighting us and all the land . . .
But Tanya's soul is not enraptured,
she feels no eagerness to go
and greet the swirling winter snow,
breathe in the hoar-frost, try to capture
some flakes to bathe her breast and face:
Tatiana dreads the icy ways.

31

The day soon comes for their departure,
belatedly, for it's high time.
The antique sleigh is checked; it's rather
decrepit, so it's cleaned of grime,
repaired and thoroughly refurbished.
The travellers are further furnished
with three kibitkas filled with pots
and pans, with mattresses, a lot
of feather beds, portmanteaus, vessels,
with chicken coops, preserves in jars,
some tables, chairs, et ceteras,
well, all the countless household chattels . . .
The footmen start to wail and cry
as eighteen nags are now brought by.

32

They're harnessed to the sleigh while servants
prepare the lunch for one and all,
pile more on the kibitkas, urgent,
excited serfs and coachmen brawl,
a bearded *postillon* is sitting
upon a jade, while serfs are flitting
towards the manor gates to sigh
and wave their mistresses goodbye.
The ladies settle down, the ancient
and creaky sleigh then slowly glides
away. "Belovéd countryside,
farewell! Farewell, secluded, silent
retreat! Will I see you again?"
Tatiana weeps with fear and pain.

33

When we at last have implemented
the dreams of the Enlightenment,
and done what Reason recommended,
(Five hundred years of argument
should be enough), our roads will surely
improve immeasurably, from poorly
constructed tracks to great chaussées
criss-crossing Russia every way;
the waters will be spanned by bridges
which stride along in mighty curves;
deep tunnels, soaring paths will serve
to cross the seas and mountain ridges –
while Christendom is sure to place
an inn on every vacant space.

34

Our roads at present are quite dreadful,
forgotten bridges slowly rot,
the awful hostelries hold beds full
of creepy-crawlies which do not
permit the weary guest a minute's
repose; not inns, but crumbling flea-pits
are what await the traveller,
in which a high-flown bill of fare
excites his hopeless, gnawing hunger.
Meanwhile a rustic Cyclops treats,
within the fire's sluggish heat,
some fragile European wonder
with clumsy Russian hammer, and
extols the potholes in this land!

35

A winter odyssey, however,
is effortless beyond compare:
as in a modish song you never
need think, a trivial affair.
Our charioteers are so attentive,
our trusty troikas most effective,
as though the mileposts flashing past
were but a fence, we move so fast;
unhappily Dame Larin, dreading
the cost of hired hacks, had used
her own dilapidated crew,
and so our heroine was heading,
distraught at her sad plight, away,
a week of boredom in a sleigh.

36

Their goal is near; before them blazing
are golden crosses, ember-bright,
on ancient cupolas; amazing,
the Moscow stonework, dazzling white!
My friends! How happy it once made me
when all the gardens, churches, belfries,
palazzos, all that lustrous show,
spread out before me, long ago.
How often when I'm separated
from you by wayward destiny,
do I evoke your memory!
Oh Moscow, Moscow — consecrated
expression of all Russian hearts,
what majesty your name imparts!

37

Surrounded by resplendent parklands
Petrovsky Castle gloomily
exults in recent glory's garlands.
Napoleon had fruitlessly,
intoxicated with his latest
success, awaited there the greatest:
for Moscow on its bended knees
to offer him the Kremlin keys.
But Moscow, not humiliated,
refused to recognise his might,
and gave him naught that could delight
his greed, instead incinerated
the town. The eager hero stayed,
surveying Moscow as it blazed.

38

Farewell, you witness to an erstwhile
renown, Petrovsky Castle! Now,
don't stop, go on, the toll-gate's meanwhile
materialised, the sledges plough
across the pot-holes, bounce and rattle
along Tverskáya Street and battle
their way past sentry boxes, lamps,
muschíks and merchants, urchins, tramps,
past boulevards and shops, Bokharans,
small shacks, tall towers, monasteries,
great palaces and pharmacies,
boutiques and coaches, kitchen gardens,
stone lions perched on fastened gates,
while on church crosses jackdaws wait.

39/40

An hour elapsed, and then another,
exhausting them, when all at once
their journey stopped beneath the cover
of worthy old St. Chariton's,
before the gateway of a mansion.
An ageing aunt who'd had consumption
for some few years, lived there. The door
was quickly opened and they saw
a shabby Kalmuck with a stocking
clasped in his hand, his caftan torn,
bespectacled, infirm and worn,
who showed them in to see the coughing
Princess ensconced on her divan:
the ladies weep, stretch out their hands.

41

"Princess, mon ange!" "Pachette!" "Alina!"
"Who would have thought?" "How many years?"
"Dear cousin! Gracious me! It's been a . . .
Oh, please! Oh, do sit down!" "And here's
my daughter, Tanya, as I told you."
"Come here, my child, and let me hold you!
How strange it is, it almost seems . . .
Well, like a novel, or a dream!
Oh Cousin, do you still remember
your Grandison?" "What? Oh, I see!
My Grandison! And where is he?"
"Right here in Moscow – in December
he called – lives by St. Simeon,
has got a newly married son.

42

"The other . . . More of him then, later,
I think. Tomorrow we must see
what can be done for Tanya, take her
to meet the waiting family.
I can't come with you, more's the pity,
can hardly walk, old age's not pretty.
But you must all be quite worn out,
we'll go to bed, that's best, no doubt!
Oh, I'm so weak, my chest is ailing,
now even pleasures are a strain,
not just the misery and pain . . .
My dears, I'm useless now, and failing . . ."
Fatigued, she took some minutes off
as she began to weep and cough.

43

The aged invalid's caresses
and pleasure move the girl, but soon
her chamber here in truth distresses
Tatiana; used to her own room,
it seems to her all most uncertain,
she cannot sleep, the silken curtain
around her bed, the pealing bells,
conspire to stop her sleeping well,
announcing chores that are approaching.
Beside the window Tanya sits,
the darkness thins and opposite
she sees not fields, but all encroaching
upon her view: a yard, and thence
a stable, kitchen and a fence.

44

And so they trundle Tanya daily
upon a circuit of soirées
to visit relatives, who gaily
observe her cool and pensive ways.
Her kin arrive from quite a distance,
call out to her at every instance,
examine her, and blithely scream:
"But you have grown, my dear! It seems
but yesterday that I looked after
my little Tanya!" "Since I held
you!" "Since I pulled your ears!" "I quelled
your squeals and heard your happy laughter!"
And then the ageing chorus sighs:
"How quickly do the years fly by!"

45

But they are utterly unaltered,
the passing years have been ignored;
Princess Eléna has not faltered,
and wears her mob cap as before,
nor powdered Aunt Lukéria Lvóvna
or lying old Lyubóv Petróvna;
Ivan Petróvich is a dolt,
Semyón Petróvich mean and cold,
while Pélagéya Nikolávna
still has her husband and her pooch,
her beau as well, monsieur Finemouche;
the husband loves his club, as ever,
is just as spineless, deaf and true,
and eats and drinks enough for two!

46

At first their daughters all embrace her,
these Moscow graces then inspect
Tatiana silently and savour
her rustic looks, the dire effect
of country life, restrained, provincial,
in some respects not very special,
in others not so bad at all;
but their defences quickly fall
and soon they're friends and paying visits
to one another, fashionably
fluff up her hair, and affably
then take one of her hands and kiss it,
while in their sing-song tones they tell
her all their girlish thoughts as well,

47

their conquests, their and others' antics,
their secrets and their childish dreams,
naïve and innocent, romantic,
though not without their crafty schemes.
Then in exchange for all the prattle
they hope to hear the tittle-tattle
of Tanya's amorous affairs.
She listens with an absent air,
remote, detached, and not replying,
nor taking in a single word,
safeguarding, as she much preferred,
the secrets of her heart, and trying
to keep her treasured joys and tears
away from all those prying ears.

48

Tatiana would like nothing more than
to share in all their 'colloquies',
and yet she finds that she is bored, and
their words so empty as to be
the most appalling stuff and nonsense,
disjointed rot in every sentence;
their conversation is so pale
that even all the slanders fail
to please, their arid questions, rumours;
the tales they tell do not display
a trace of wit or brain all day,
not even by a fluke. No humour
invigorates our upper crust,
their follies, too, are dry as dust.

49

The dandies from the Foreign Office
look down on Tanya priggishly;
they see in her a naïve novice
and speak of her quite frigidly;
one melancholy toff, reposing
against a door-post is composing
an elegy in which she's styled
"Ideal"; Vyazémski's nicely whiled
away a wearisome reception
at some dull aunt's, which proved a strain,
by keeping her well entertained;
and glancing round in her direction
an old roué both smiles and prates,
while making sure his wig sits straight.

50

But where Melpomene's incessant
laments and wailing still resound,
there where she flaunts her iridescent
attire before a frosty crowd,
where hushed Thalía gently dozes,
disdaining praise, bouquets and roses,
and young, adoring devotees
admire alone Terpsichore
(just as it was when we, her patrons,
were simply fresh-faced revellers)
there youthful men's binoculars,
lorgnettes of haughty, jealous matrons
ignore Tatiana, one and all,
both in the boxes and the stalls.

51

She's taken down to the *Sobránie,*
with its shrill music, noise and heat,
excitement, candles, and the carefree
light-hearted dancers' whirling feet,
the scantly clad young beauties glowing,
the galleries quite overflowing
with motley folk, while in an arc
stand would-be brides to make their mark.
All this at once inflames the senses:
accomplished fops are on display,
their waistcoats and their saucy ways
and negligent lorgnettes; pretentious
hussars on leave haste gleaming by
or try to catch a lady's eye.

52

Resplendent are the starry vistas
of Moscow nights, its maidens, too . . .
Yet brighter than her stellar sisters
is Luna in the gauzy blue . . .
But she I dare not try petition
in song, whose regal apparition
amongst the ladies and the girls
alone illumines all in pearl . . .
With what celestial pride she brushes
the earth! How sensuous her breast!
How wondrously her gaze now rests,
how languidly . . . Enough! It touches
my heart too deeply . . . Cease, oh cease!
With folly I have made my peace . . .

53

The guests all bow, guffaw and scurry,
mazurka, waltz are what they dance;
beside a column in the flurry
Tatiana stands between two aunts,
remaining still and quite unnoticed;
she looks around, her eyes unfocussed,
detesting all the haste and din.
She almost chokes – and soon is in
a reverie of country habits,
of villages and sparkling brooks,
of fields and flowers, quiet nooks,
her books and novels, for a minute
the shady avenue of limes
where *he* appeared from time to time.

54

Thus lost in her sad meditation
she disregards the pomp and noise;
a man, awash with admiration,
repeatedly observes her poise.
On seeing this imposing soldier,
a general, the aunts grow bolder
and, nudging Tanya with their arms,
they whisper, hardly keeping calm,
"Look carefully, but without gawking,
there on your left!" "My left? But where?"
"It doesn't matter! Over there,
in uniform, that pair, they're talking . . .
He's moved off now . . . Look, if you can!"
"The general? That bloated man?"

55

So now we'll offer our best wishes
to Tanya, and then pause; but let
me say some words before I finish
to make quite sure I don't forget
the friend of whom I sing . . . So saying,
I'll do it now without delaying:
"I sing a friend who's noble, true,
his many quirks and foibles, too,
so bless my wearisome exertions
oh thou, my epic muse, I pray,
give me my staff, let me not stray."
At last! I've paid with this excursion
my debt to Classicism. Great!
To prologues, too, if rather late!

CHAPTER EIGHT

Fare thee well, and if for ever,
Still for ever, fare thee well.
                              Byron

CHAPTER EIGHT

1

In fledgling days when I was flowering
serenely in the verdant grounds
of my Lyceum and devouring
Apuleius, (although I frowned
on Cicero), that was the moment
from when in secret dales, in lucent
flamboyant Spring amid the cry
of swans on sparkling lakes nearby,
there in those magic, silent places
the Muse at first appeared to me.
My schoolboy's room was suddenly
aglow: the Muse displayed her graces,
she sang of childish dreams, of old
acclaim, and troubles of the soul.

2

The world received her, blithely smiling,
and growing fame made us feel brave;
Derzhávin found us quite beguiling,
and blessing us, went to his grave.

. . . .
. . . .
. . . .
. . . .
. . . .
. . . .
. . . .
. . . .
. . . .
. . . .

3

So making arbitrary feelings
the only law which I obeyed,
I led my Muse into the reeling
excitement of our mad affrays
and feasts, so hated by the nightly
patrols; she brought her gifts to wildly
abandoned, crazy revelling,
bacchante-like she loved to sing
to guests who were all blithely drinking.
When I was young and fancy-free,
the crowd would follow her and me,
all dancing, prancing, gay, unthinking,
and I was proud when friends espied
my fickle mistress at my side.

4

But then I left my erstwhile fellows
and fled afar . . . She came along
and eased my silent way with mellow,
bewitching secret tales and songs.
How often on Caucasian hillsides,
like Leonore, in the moonlight,
she'd travel with me on a horse.
How often on grim Tauris' shores
she led me in the murky darkness
to listen to the steady sigh
of waves, the Nereids' sad cry,
the deep, resounding, ceaseless chorus
of billows breaking as they fall
and praise the Maker of us all.

5

The glitter and the brash excesses
of distant cities left behind,
she visited the wild recesses
of sad Moldavia to find
the humble home and tents of vagrant,
untutored tribes; now wild and errant,
she swapped the language of the gods
for ballads of the steppes, for odds
and ends of alien, exotic
expressions, all of which were dear
to her. And then my muse appeared,
an artless country miss, nostalgic,
within my garden, in her hands
she had a book, a French romance.

6

Now for the first time I am taking
my muse with me to a soirée.
Suspiciously and almost shaking
with jealousy, I watch the way
my rural maid behaves. She lightly
meanders through a crowd of tightly
congested callers: envoys, then
proud ladies, haughty gentlemen,
and military fops . . . Demurely
she takes a seat and looks about,
admires the sparkling, boisterous crowd,
the men in tails, who, moving surely
towards their hostess, form a frame
around the girls and stately dames.

7

She likes the vibrant, measured order
of oligarchic colloquies,
the chill of icy pride affords her
delight, as do the stiff grandees
of every age and rank. One moment!
Who's that, so nebulous and silent?
He seems a stranger to them, though . . .
Before him faces come and go
like irritating apparitions.
What is it – wounded pride or spleen
upon his face? Is it – *Eugene*?
What does he want? Is he a vision?
Can it be him? It is, I fear!
Since when, I pray, has he been here?

8

I wonder if the man's politer?
What sort of mask will he display?
Is he the same eccentric blighter,
or will he act another way?
What guise will he take on? A bigot?
A Quaker? Patriot? Or Melmoth?
A Harold? A sophisticate?
Or will he simply imitate
some other type? Or might he even
turn out to be a decent soul,
like everybody on the whole?
Give up a pose that's out of season?
He's fooled us all with tricks and show!
You know him, then? – Well, yes and no!

9

But why are you so very hostile
when you refer to him? Maybe
because we love a really facile
opinion? Criticise with glee?
Because the ardour of a zealous
enthusiast makes small fry jealous?
Because wit's love of freedom thwarts
the dull? Because we're often caught
confusing word and deed too gladly,
because stupidity is grim
and whimsical? Because the dim
and dour take petty trifles (sadly)
too gravely, and nonentity
suits tiny minds just perfectly?

10

Thrice blest is he whose youth was youthful,
and blest is he who's turned out shrewd,
who's learned with time to make life fruitful,
and bear life's chill with fortitude,
who's never followed dreams or passions,
who's never scorned the rabble's fashions,
at twenty was a fop or blade,
at thirty married to a maid
with money, rid himself, aged fifty,
of all his multifarious debts,
is solidly and smoothly set
upon the road to fame, which swiftly
proceeds from wealth. The world then can
proclaim, "Now, *there's* a splendid man!"

11

But it is sad to think no purpose
was served by all our youthful days,
that we betrayed them, made them worthless,
that they, too, duped us in their way,
that all our very best endeavours,
our fresh-faced day-dreams have for ever
decayed like leaves in rotting mounds
when autumn wafts them to the ground;
how odious the thought of eating,
and drinking toasts unendingly,
life as a mere formality,
saluting toffs at genteel meetings
with whom one does not even share
a thought or feeling anywhere.

12

And if the prattling moral classes
make one the target of critique,
it's quite outrageous if one passes
(you will agree that it's a cheek)
oneself off as a fake eccentric,
a tragic, crazed and wild hysteric,
or some infernal, loathsome beast,
or my own 'Demon' at the least!
Eugene (returning to my hero
again), since having killed his friend,
and never having to attend
to duties, twenty-six now, shallow,
disinterested, without a wife,
had nothing which could fill his life.

13

Consumed by irksome agitation,
a craving for a change of air,
(a most unpleasant situation,
a cross which is most hard to bear),
he'd left his dwelling in the country,
the solitude of woods and sundry
delightful meadows all in bud,
but haunted daily now with blood,
and then he'd set off on his journey
with but one memory throughout,
had travelled aimlessly about,
till all the world seemed dull and weary . . .
Returning, he had gone to call,
like Chatski, straight from boat to ball.

14

And then! The gathering grew restless,
a murmur rustled through the crowd,
a lady walked towards her hostess,
a general, imposing, proud,
escorting her . . . Not cold, nor hurried,
not talkative, pretentious, flurried,
she was without unpleasant quirks,
without a haughty glance or smirk
and lacked annoying artifices,
nor did she flaunt her eminence,
avoiding giving all offence,
restrained, unconscious of her riches,
a paradigm *du comme il faut* . . .
What's that in Russian? I don't know!

217

15

The other ladies all moved closer
to her, the older women smiled,
the gentlemen bowed low and lower,
and tried to catch her gaze meanwhile.
The maidens hushed as they passed by her,
and none held nose, or shoulders, higher
than he who ushered her along,
the general. It would be wrong
to claim she was a striking beauty,
but no one could have found a trace
of anything in gait or face,
her gown or bearing, which the snooty
and autocratic London crew
call "vulgar". (How I wish I knew

16

the Russian for that word, but sadly
again I simply can't translate
the term, for it is looked on badly
by us; it's only come of late
to our domains, and yet I like it –
Some wit will doubtless be delighted
with it in quips . . .). But let's return
to our *belle dame*, whom we discern
with lovely Nina Voronskýa,
the Neva's Cleopatra, at
a table; I'm quite certain that
you'd not have found more to admire
in Nina's dazzling marble glow
than her companion put on show.

17

"Can that be her?" Onegin wonders,
"Can it be . . . ? Surely not!" he feels.
"What, from the rustic backwoods yonder . . .?"
With his lorgnette he quickly steals
a glance at her, and then another . . .
He has a fancy he can't smother,
that those forgotten features cast
a faded shadow from the past . . .
"Excuse me, Prince, but with the Spanish
ambassador, that lady there . . .
the red beret . . . ?" The prince then stares
at him. "Of course, you've been long banished
from Petersburg and social life.
I'll introduce you. She's my wife."

18

"You're married, then!" "Yes, to a charmer."
"How long's it been?" "About two years."
"To whom?" "The Larin girl." "Tatiana!"
"You know her?" "Yes, I live quite near
the family." "Let's go and meet her."
The prince goes to his wife and leads her
to face his relative and friend.
The princess stares, but in the end
preserves her poise, and whatsoever
has stirred her soul, however great
her agitation, she placates
her torments, taking care she never
betrays her thoughts; her calm maintained,
her bow is gracious and restrained.

19

Forsooth! Well well! It was not merely
that Tanya didn't flinch, go red,
turn deathly pale, nor did she clearly
reveal surprise. It must be said,
indeed, that she remained unmoving,
no eyebrow twitched or looked reproving;
and though he stared quite carefully,
try as he would, he couldn't see
a trace of Tanya as he'd known her.
He tried to chat . . . but seemed struck dumb;
she asked politely whence he'd come,
if he'd been home, was still a loner.
Then looking bored, she turned around . . .
and left him rooted to the ground.

20

Can that be Tanya, can it truly
be her, the pure girl at the start
of this our tale, the one to whom he'd
held forth in distant country parts,
had moralised in righteous fervour,
had preached propriety and order,
from whom he had a letter where
she'd laid her deepest feelings bare?
That chaste young girl – is it a vision? –
whose passion had been unrestrained,
that chaste young girl whom he'd disdained
because of her obscure position;
can it be she, now so urbane,
is *she* the one he's seen again?

21

He leaves the glittering assembly
and pensively goes home to rest.
His dreams that evening, both unfriendly
and pleasurable, leave him distressed.
When he awakes, there is a letter
awaiting him. He soon feels better:
Prince N. *'entreats his company
at a soirée.'* A chance to see
Tatiana! "God be praised! How pleasing!
I'll go, I'll go!" And so he pens
a gentlemanly note – and then –
What's wrong with him? Why is he feeling
so strange? Is it conceit or ire?
Does his dead soul now know – desire?

22

Once more he counts the hours and minutes,
and wishes night would soon arrive . . .
The clock strikes ten. His wait is finished,
so he sets out upon the drive
to meet the princess. Tense, tormented,
he finds Tatiana unattended
and sits down with her for a while,
but words won't come, he cannot smile
and barely, sounding almost distant,
replies to her polite remarks;
his head is bursting with a dark
and strange, unlooked-for yet persistent
idea . . . He now at last can see
that she is quite at ease, and free.

23

The prince comes in, thus terminating
the mortifying tête-à-tête;
the two of them are soon relating
their youthful pranks when they first met,
and as they're laughing more guests enter . . .
The gleeful gossip starts to centre
around the spicy malice which
makes high society so rich.
But near the Princess all the prattle
consisted of mere balderdash,
though free of show; sometimes a splash
of sense disturbed the tittle-tattle,
but bare of 'deathless truths' and thought,
without affronts of any sort.

24

Our capital's most winsome flowers
were here, both great nobility
and paragons of fashion, towers
of all that we expect to see,
and everywhere the same old faces,
the fools one needs in all such places,
the ancient ladies sitting there
in mobcaps, roses in their hair,
and looking evil; several spinsters,
severe and grim, an envoy here,
discussing statecraft loud and clear,
and there an ageing white-haired mister
was cracking ageing jokes which now
seem dull and out of date somehow.

25

And here a gentleman who hated
the whole wide world: in epigrams
the too-sweet tea was execrated,
the ladies' platitudes were damned,
bemedalled sisters with their chatter,
a foolish tale that didn't matter,
the other men, reviews of books,
the war, the snow, his own wife's looks.
— — — — — — — — — — — — — — — — — — — —
— — — — — — — — — — — — — — — — — — — —
— — — — — — — — — — — — — — — — — — — —
— — — — — — — — — — — — — — — — — — — —
— — — — — — — — — — — — — — — — — — — —
— — — — — — — — — — — — — — — — — — — —

26

And there's Prolázov, who'd distinguished
himself for brutishness of heart,
whom you, Saint-Priest, have often relished
as target of your comic art;
and in the door another tyrant
of ballrooms stood and stared, as strident
as prints in fashion magazines,
a rosy and cherubic sheen
upon his face, immobile, silent,
and tightly laced; a traveller
who'd just arrived, a bachelor
whose starchy collar and deportment
incited glances from the guests,
who saw in him a pompous pest.

27

Yet my Onegin spent the evening
obsessed with Tanya quite alone;
not with the little, self-demeaning
and smitten girl he once had known,
but with a princess, cold and distant,
a goddess who remained resistant
to prayers, a proud divinity
who is the Neva's majesty . . .
Oh Humankind! You also follow
your forebear – Eve: quite insecure,
you're tempted by the serpent's lure
to the forbidden tree, you also
demand the outlawed fruit, without
which Eden's worth is cancelled out.

28

But how Tatiana now is altered!
How well she plays her stately role!
Not one brief instant has she faltered,
remaining fully in control
and utterly at ease. Whoever
would dare to think this regal, clever,
collected woman, this splendid queen
of the salons had really been
the tender girl whose heart he'd shaken,
when in the moonlit hours of night
just as her soul was taking flight
into the arms of sleep, she'd waken,
imagining life at his side,
a future as his loving bride.

29

No matter whether young or grizzled,
we all fall victim to love's sway;
indeed, its whims are beneficial:
like stormy fields on springtime days,
hearts freshen in the rain of passion,
return to life, renewed, refashioned,
as new-found vigour drives the shoots
to burgeon into luscious fruits . . .
In later years when we are wasted,
our fires extinguished as we age,
no longer splendid blooms, but sage,
how sad the thought of what we've tasted,
as autumn storms transform the leas
to marshland, while they strip the trees.

30

There is no doubt Eugene now madly,
alas! loves Tanya like some boy.
Consumed with passion, he now gladly
spends day and night, aglow with joy . . .
Ignoring promptings from his conscience
he drives up daily to the entrance
of her *palais*, where he will wait,
or chase her like some roving shade.
He's happy at the simple notion
of being able, now and then,
to touch her arm or hand and, when
required, adjust her boa, motion
retainers to one side while he
picks up her kerchief blissfully.

31

However much he tries and struggles,
she does not even notice him;
receiving him at home, unruffled,
she bows at times, polite and prim,
or drops a word as she's departing,
then leaves him standing, dazed and smarting;
she's free of all that coquetry
so censured by society.
Onegin's starting to grow ashen,
she does not see him, does not care,
he's losing heart and near despair,
as if consumptive, failing, waxen.
Physicians chorus in alarm:
a spa would do Eugene no harm!

32

He does not go. He would much rather
inform his forebears that he soon
would join them in the grave. Tatiana
(for such is woman) neither swoons
nor does she even see or worry.
But he is stubborn, in a hurry,
not having given up all hope
(a sick man has no time to mope),
he dashes off an ardent letter
to her with feeble hand, although
he found notes silly, and we know
just what he meant. That didn't fetter
his zeal, so greatly was he stirred,
and here's his missive – word for word.

Onegin's Letter to Tatiana

"I see it all! You'll be upset
at my sad secret's revelation.
What bitter, scornful condemnation
your eyes will speak, to my regret . . .
But what, in truth, is my intention
in laying bare my soul to you?
And what contemptuous inventions
will I now give occasion to?

"When chance initially dictated
that we should meet, you radiated
a sort of simple tenderness,
although I never quite perceived it
as yet unready to believe it . . .
And then I wanted nothing less
than unrestricted independence,
a freedom I've since learned to hate.
There also was my true repentance
for wretched Lenski's tragic fate . . .
I left behind all that I treasure,
confusing fun with liberty;
My God! How foolish can one be!
And I've been punished in full measure!

"But now! To see you night and day,
to follow you where'er you wander,
with loving looks to catch the play
of your dear eyes, your mouth, not squander
a word you say, to understand
with all my soul your full perfection,
to melt with woes before you, and
grow pale, and pine, – in your affection . . .

"What bliss! Yet lost to me, I fear . . .
For you I drag my abject being
at random; minutes, hours are dear
to me, which I now waste, while seeing
my future as a lonely trial,
unhappy, brutish, short and vile.
I know my days on earth are numbered,
and should I really wish to stay
alive, I cannot always wonder
if I shall see you, come the day.

"I dread that you will now imagine
a ruse concealed within my plea,
despicable, and quite unbidden,
profaning your integrity,
once more I hear your condemnation . . .
Yet if you knew the cruel pain
of thirsting for your approbation,
of burning love, time and again
of stilling agitated feelings
and clutching wildly after you,
or frenzied, bathed in tears, of kneeling
and pouring out appeals, of new
avowals, groans, and yet keep feigning
reserve in gesture, speech and gaze,
conversing in such diverse ways,
while glancing at you uncomplaining . . .

As fate decrees, so let it be!
My struggle's finally completed,
my inner strength has been defeated,
to you I leave my destiny."

33

There's no reply. Another letter.
Again no answer. Then a third,
and this one also fares no better.
Eugene drives off, still undeterred,
to a soirée, where proud and stately
she nears, approaching him sedately;
austere, she passes by, neglects
to notice him, does not direct
a single word to him. How frosty
she is. How hard those stubborn lips
attempt to keep a steadfast grip
upon her wrath. Eugene looks closely
for tears, solicitude, unease . . .
But no! For rage is all he sees . . .

34

and probably some trepidation
lest husband or society
recall a former assignation,
still fresh in Eugene's memory . . .
There was no hope. So he, still cursing
his folly, drove away, while nursing
the madness in his heart. He then
renounced the world, and once again
remembered in his book-lined study
the time when cruel, ruthless spleen
had plucked him from the social scene
and far away from everybody,
had locked him for a lengthy spell
deep in some awful rural hell.

35

His books now occupied him wholly,
he glanced at Gibbon and Rousseau,
then Herder, Chamfort, and Manzoni,
Madame de Staël, Bichat, Tissot.
Nor did he slight our Russian writers,
read weighty tomes, and also lighter,
skimmed through the works of Fontenelle,
perused the sceptic Bayle as well,
rejecting nothing, deep or shallow,
not magazines, nor almanacs,
which sermonise or launch attacks
on me, describing me as callow,
or sing my praises now and then,
e sempre bene, gentlemen!

36

Although his eyes were quickly skimming
the page, his thoughts were far away;
desires and dreams and woes were brimming
within his head in disarray.
He read and read, kept persevering,
between the lines there kept appearing
quite different lines, which left his eyes,
his mind and feelings mesmerised:
mysterious legends and traditions,
passed down through aeons by the heart,
strange dreams his senses couldn't chart,
forebodings, rumours and suspicions,
or novels boring through and through,
or maidens' maudlin *billet-doux*.

37

And then a kind of slow stagnation
comes over him and dulls his thoughts,
and to his mind Imagination
deals out a hand of cards . . . of sorts:
he either sees, as if reposing
upon the melting snow and dozing
a youth, and then he hears with dread
a voice remark, "Well, well, he's dead."
Or else he finds long-gone detractors,
base cowards and old enemies,
young ladies famed for treacheries,
departed, charming malefactors,
or he espies a country place
and at a window sees . . . *her* face.

38

He grew so used to wholly losing
himself in studies, that he soon
almost went off his head with musing
or else became (oh, what a boon!)
a poet. Potent magnetism
assisted with the mechanism
of Russian verses, which my daft
and addled pupil nearly grasped.
How much a poet he resembled
we see when he would sit alone
before the hearth and warm his bones,
hum 'Benedetta', all but tremble
at 'Idol mio', drop a shoe
into the flames, or some review.

39

The days rushed by. As for the snow, it
receded as the Spring drew nigh.
He did not turn into a poet,
did not go mad, nor did he die.
He leaves his rooms, exhilarated,
where, marmot-like, he'd hibernated,
deserts his double-windows, books,
his cosy, cloistered inglenook,
and one enchanting morning hurries
along the Neva in his sleigh.
On glinting ice the sun now plays,
the snow is tossed in muddy flurries
through all the lanes and thoroughfares,
now chock-a-block with slush; but where's

40

Onegin gone? I can't help feeling
that you have guessed it instantly.
Quite right! For now we find him stealing
away to *her*, whom he must see:
Tatiana. Quite unchanged and heartsick,
my friend walks in, the same eccentric,
and almost like a corpse. The hall
is bare, reception rooms, and all
the others . . . Empty! Then he opens
a door . . . What strikes him with such force?
The Princess! God – it's she, of course,
alone, subdued, in tears and broken,
and with a letter that she's read . . .
her hand supports her mournful head.

41

Her silent pain – and oh! – her torment . . .
The long-gone Tanya – It is she!
Who could have failed, just at this moment,
to read the truth? Onegin sees
her as she'd been, a simple maiden,
his heart is beating, overladen
and bursting with regret. Eugene
has fallen at her feet, she's seen
him now, looks up before proceeding,
without annoyance or surprise,
observes the dead look in his eyes,
his censure mute, his features pleading . . .
She dreams of how things were before,
and is a simple girl once more.

42

She does not bid him rise, nor does she
withdraw her look from his sad eyes,
nor move her hand, which he holds closely
upon his lips with ardent sighs.
What is she sadly contemplating . . . ?
She's silent now . . . reflective, waiting,
and then she softly says to him:
"Enough. Get up. I'll not be prim
or harsh, but speak to you quite plainly.
Onegin, tell me, do you still
recall the garden where fate willed
that we should meet, and I, ungainly
and humble, heard your homily?
Well, now it's my turn to be free.

43

"Onegin, I was then still youthful,
and was, I dare say, fairer, too.
I loved you deeply, to be truthful . . .
But what occurred, what did you do?
How did you treat my girlish boldness?
With harsh severity and coldness.
For there was nothing – was there? – good
about a meek girl's love you could
find novel. God! It still affects me
when I remember your cold stare,
your reprimand, though I don't care
for blame, as you behaved correctly,
were right about me, very shrewd,
for that I owe you gratitude.

44

"But *there*, in that far-off and lonely
provincial house, remote from all
opprobrium, I was too homely
for you . . . or not? – So why this fall
from protocol, this adoration?
Perhaps the friendly veneration
that one and all confer on me,
my standing in society,
impress you now? My wealth? The kindness
the Court has shown us? Or my brave,
good husband and the blood he gave?
Or could it simply be a mindless
attempt to bring about my shame
and you a monstrous sort of fame?

45

"I'm weeping now . . . Have you forgotten
your Tanya of that long-gone day?
If not, then know: the misbegotten,
unfeeling, stern and scornful way
you lectured me . . . Had I the power,
I'd rather see your awful glower
than all those tears, the notes you've sent.
I find them quite impertinent!
At least you then showed real compassion
for me. But why must you behave
as if you were a lowly slave
and fall before me in this fashion?
How can a noble heart and mind
descend to follies of this kind?

46

"And yet, Onegin, all the splendour,
the glitter of this loathsome world . . .
How gladly I would now surrender
my triumphs and this gaudy swirl,
my splendid house, and all the functions,
I'd give them up without compunction . . .
Oh, what does it all mean to me,
the fumes, the noise, the frippery . . . ?
. . . To see my books, my garden haven
and my old haunts, my humble home,
where we first met, where I would roam,
the churchyard with its simply graven
memorial, where trees in bloom
protect my nurse's shady tomb.

47

"Perhaps my marriage was too hurried,
for happiness was near . . . My fate
is sealed. My mother, tearful, worried,
entreated me . . . it's now too late . . .
To Tanya it no longer mattered,
her future seemed completely shattered . . .
And now you must, I beg you, go,
for in your heart you are, I know,
a man of dignity and virtue.
Onegin! Why should I pretend?
I love you still, and to the end
of time . . . I have no wish to hurt you . . .
But I'm another's faithful wife,
with him I'll spend my married life."

48

She's gone! As if a bolt of thunder
had struck him, he can only stare;
it seems his heart has burst asunder
as tempests clamour everywhere.
But suddenly he hears the jingle
of spurs; his nerves begin to tingle,
Tatiana's husband then appears.
Yet we, dear reader, must, I fear,
just at this most unhappy moment
forsake our hero where he stood . . .
And how long for? – Ah, me! For good!
We've followed him up to the present,
and have – Hurrah! – now reached the shore.
We needn't journey any more!

49

Whoe'er you are, my gentle reader,
be you a friend or enemy,
it's time to part, it's really been a
delight to share your company.
Farewell! And may you find whatever
you've searched for in my poor endeavour:
tumultuous remembrances,
relief from work's encumbrances,
keen images, or faults of grammar,
God grant that you may find a crumb
of food for relaxation, some
refreshment for the heart, some glamour,
or fare for battles in reviews . . .
Now let me say farewell to you!

50

And you, my strange companion, also:
Adieu! And my adored ideal
as well, and you, my modest cantos,
my little work which has revealed
to me what every poet envies:
oblivion of worldly frenzies,
while chatting happily with friends.
How many days I've had to spend
as time rushed by, since Tanya's vision,
Onegin's, too, appeared to me,
a hazy dream . . . I could not see
their future story with precision,
not even through a magic glass
foretell what then would come to pass.

51

Of those to whom I first recited
my verse at happy gatherings,
my comrades whom they so delighted,
as Persia's Sadi loved to sing,
"A few are absent, some departed."
Yet I have finished what I started . . .
Onegin's portrait . . . Also she
is there, whose dear identity
produced "Tatiana" . . . Fate has taken
so much: good friends who've not remained
at life's great feast, who have not drained
their cups, who have by now forsaken
life's narrative, as you have seen
me leave my cherished friend – Eugene.

NOTES

The Master Motto

Apparently written by Pushkin himself, the passage translates as follows:

> Filled with vanity, he had even more of that kind of pride which allows a person, from a – perhaps illusory – sense of superiority, to admit to both his good and bad deeds with the same indifference.
>
> Taken from a personal letter

Dedication

Pletnev (1792–1862), a scholar and Professor of Russian Literature at St. Petersburg University from 1832 and friend of the Pushkin family.

Notes on Chapter 1

Motto

'to live it hurries and to feel it hastes . . .'

This is preceded in the original by the line

'O'er life thus glides young ardour,'

which Pushkin omitted, but makes the meaning clearer.

Sonnet 2

Ruslan and Ludmila: A mock epic poem by Pushkin (1820).
though now I really hate the North: Written in Bessarabia (Pushkin's note).

Sonnet 3

Letny Park: A summer park on the banks of the Neva.

Sonnet 12

Faublas: Hero of a novel by Louvet de Couvrai (1760–97). A seducer of other men's wives.

Sonnet 15

bolivar: Hat à la Bolivar (Pushkin's note) A broad-brimmed black top hat, the height of Fashion in the Paris and St. Petersburg of the 1820s. Named after the South American liberator.
Bréguet: Celebrated French watchmaker. The reference here is clearly to one of his repeaters.

Sonnet 16

Talon's: A well known French restaurant in St. Petersburg (Pushkin's note).
Kavérin: Man-about-town, hussar and friend of Pushkin.

Sonnet 17

Phaedra, Moena, Cleopatra: Heroines of various plays, operas and ballets popular in the St. Petersburg of the time.

Sonnet 18

A magic world: Refers to the theatre at the turn of the century.
Fonvízin (1745–92): Satirist.
Knyazhnín (1742–91), *Oeróv* (1769–1816), *Katénin* (1792–1852): authors of tragedies in the French style.
Sémyonóva (1786–1849): Shakespearean actress also known for her performances in Russian plays.
Sháhovskóy (1777–1846): Author of comedies in the French style.
Didelot (1767–1837): French choreographer and ballet master engaged at the St. Petersburg ballet.

Sonnet 20

Istomina (1799–1848): A pupil of Didelot and a famous ballerina, to whom Pushkin had been attracted.

Sonnet 24

Grimm (1723–1807): French encylopedist. Pushkin in his notes adds a quotation from Rousseau's *Confessions*, and remarks that "Grimm was well ahead of his time, for nowadays people in the whole of enlightened Europe clean their nails with a special brush."

Sonnet 25

A fop: In the original Eugene is referred to as 'a second . . .' and the name is omitted. The reference, however, is to Pyotor Chadáev (1793–1856), a philosopher and dandy, and friend of Pushkin. One of Chadáev's writings, published in 1836, caused the author to be officially declared insane.

Sonnet 33

Armida: Derived from the French, a name given to a woman of independent spirit who unites beauty, grace and seductiveness.

Sonnet 42

J.B. Say: French economist (1767–1832).
Jeremy Bentham: English philosopher and jurist(1748–1832).
Both were popular subjects of discussion in intellectual circles of the time. Pushkin comments in a note: 'This whole stanza is nothing more than a most subtle compliment to our fair countrywomen . . . who combine enlightenment with amiability, and that strict purity of morals with an Oriental charm, which so enchanted Mme de Staël (*Dix ans d'exil*).'

Sonnet 48

. . . as the poet sang some years before: A derisive reference to the lyric poem *To the Goddess of the Neva* by Murayov (1757–1807).

the Mil'onnaya: 'Million Street', running parallel to the Neva, and one block removed from it.

Tasso: Italian poet (1544–95).

Sonnet 49

Adria: the Adriatic.

Brenta: River flowing into the Adriatic near Venice.

Albion's lyre: Reference to Byron's poetry.

Sonnet 50

the heights: Written in Odessa (Pushkin's note). Nabokov speculates about the exact meaning of this passage, and suggests that Pushkin perhaps had 'in mind the elevation of the Odessa seashore'. This speculation would appear to be borne out by a painting I have 'discovered' by Ivan Aivazovsky (*View of Odessa by Moonlight*. 1846.), which readers with Internet access can find at the following www.abcgallery.com/A/aivazovsky/aivazovsky10.html and which impressively illustrates what Nabokov means.

the skies of Africa: Reference to Pushkin's great-grandfather, abducted at the age of seven from the coast of Africa and taken to Constantinople, where he was rescued by the Russian envoy and presented as a gift to Peter the Great. He was baptised, sent abroad to undertake military studies, and eventually became a general, dying at the age of almost ninety in 1781. Pushkin was very proud of his African ancestry.

Sonnet 57

Salgir: A river near Bakhchissarai, a Tartar town and one-time residence of the khans of the Crimea. The references are to two of Pushkin's poems, the Caucasian girl in *The Caucasian Captive* and the harem girls in *The Fountain of Bakhchissarai*.

Notes on Chapter 2

Motto

A pun. In Horace the word means 'Oh countryside', while the second 'Oh Rus!' refers to the old name for Russia.

Sonnet 4

what his serfs were forced to pay: Serfs were normally required to provide the master with unpaid labour. Onegin, by asking a small rent instead, showed himself to be an enlightened landowner.

Sonnet 5

A Mason!: Freemasonry was considered to be a home of liberal thought, and so a landowner with such affiliations would be regarded as a dangerous revolutionary.

Sonnet 8

The last five lines of this stanza were originally omitted by Pushkin, probably because he feared trouble with the censor.

Sonnet 12

"Oh come into my golden hall . . ." Aria from a forgotten comic opera very popular in Russia during the first part of the 19th century, adapted by the forgotten Krasnopolski from a Viennese original by the equally forgotten Kauer.

Sonnet 17

Passion: Not only matters of the heart, but also feelings such as hatred, jealousy, and greed.

Sonnet 24

this name: i.e. Tatiana, as 'the most euphonious Greek names, such as, for instance, Agathon, Philetus, Theodora, Thecla, and so forth, are used with us only among the common people.' (Pushkin's note)

Sonnet 30

Lovelace: A handsome dashing rake from Richardson's *Clarissa*.
Grandison: Sir Charles Grandison, title of a novel by Richardson. Grandison is a 'Good Man', a masculine counterpart to *Pamela* and *Clarissa*, and thus the very opposite to 'her Grandison' from the conclusion of the stanza.

Sonnet 32

shaved serfs intended for the army: Serfs intended by their masters to join the army had their forelocks shaved in order to make them easily recognisable.

Sonnet 33

. . . sometimes deign to call 'Prashkovia' 'Paulina': (Mrs.) Prashkovia was a common Russian feminine name, which the youthful Mrs. Larin frenchified to 'Paulina', as in chapter 7, sonnet 41, line 1 the Russian 'Pasha' is frenchified to 'Pachette'.

Sonnet 35

the Larins wept on their bouquet: According to Nabokov, on Trinity Day 'the tradition is that a person must shed as many tears for his sins as there are dew-drops . . . on the bouquet of flowers' he or she brings to church.
kvas: Russian soft drink, sometimes slightly fermented.

Sonnet 36

a second crown: 'The aura of a good man's death' (Nabokov). The first crown was held over the bridegroom's head at his wedding by the best man.

Sonnet 37

his medal: In the original the 'Ochakov decoration', a medal commemorating the taking of the Ochakov fortress on the Black Sea in 1788.

Notes on Chapter 3

Motto

'She was a girl, she was in love.'

Sonnet 2

Phyllis: Generalised name for a country maiden, often found in 'Arcadian' poetry.

Sonnet 3

The dots indicate lines cancelled by Pushkin.

Sonnet 5

Svetlana: A reference to the famous eponymous ballad by Zhukovski, (1812): 'Dear Svetlana sat sad and silent . . . by the window'.

Sonnet 9

Julie Wolmar: heroine of Rousseau's novel, *Julie, ou la nouvelle Héloïse*, 1761.
Malek-Adhel: fictitious dashing Muslim general and warrior from the 12th century. Hero of *Mathilde*: 1805, a novel by Sophie Cottin.

de Linar: forceful, dark-haired Swedish lover of *Valérie*, in the novel of the same name by Mme de Krüdener (1803).

Werther: Tragic hero, who commits suicide, of Goethe's *Die Leiden des jungen Werthers*, 1774.

Grandison: 'a good man', (hence the description of him as 'wearisome'), hero of Richardson's novel of 1754, *Sir Charles Grandison*. In *Eugene Onegin* he is contrasted with *Lovelace*, the dashing, handsome rake of Richardson's *Clarissa* (1748–9). Also see the note to Chapter 2, sonnet 30.

Sonnet 10

Clarissa: see above.

Delphine: A widow of 21, who is engaged in a love affair with a married man, main figure in a novel of 1802 by Mme de Staël. Nabokov comments; 'If the moribund *Werther* and *Julie* are still readable today – in a detached mood of study, at least – Mme de Staël is not endurable under any circumstances.'

Julie: see above, sonnet 9.

Sonnet 12

Ahasver: The Wandering Jew, condemned to roam the world for ever, having refused to help Christ on the way to Calvary. Other accounts say he laughed at Christ on his way to be crucified. An important figure in European literature, transformed during the Romantic era into a sort of Byronic hero. Pushkin probably got to know of him through Byron's *Childe Harold*, among other sources. Wagner's *Der fliegende Holländer* and *Tannhäuser* are among the best known later renderings of the figure.

Sbogar: a blond Dalmatian brigand, hero of *Jean Sbogar*, a novel by Charles Nodier (1818).

Melmoth: Hero of *Melmoth, ou l'Homme errant*, another gloomy wayfarer, from a novel by C.R. Maturin (*Melmoth the Wanderer*, 1820), an Irish clergyman, and translated into French.

the pensive Vampire: reference to Byron's *The Vampire, A Tale* (1819), also translated into French. *The Corsair*: the poem by Byron (1813), known to Pushkin in French translation.

Sonnet 13

Phoebus: Another name for Apollo, the Greek god of light and the arts.

Sonnet 29

Bógdanóvich I.F. (1743–1803): Minor Russian poet.
Parny: Chevalier de Parny: (1753–1815), French poet particularly fond of the words 'tendre' and 'tendresse'.

Sonnet 30

Baratinski: Russian poet and soldier (1800–1844), stationed in Finland, whose best known work is *The Feasts* (1820), in which he expresses admiration for Pushkin, although later disliking EO.

Sonnet 32

wafer: A personal seal, stuck to the folded letter.

Notes on Chapter 4

Motto

'Morality is in the nature of things'.

Sonnet 26

Chateaubriand (1768–1848) François-René, French writer, especially renowned for his descriptions of nature, especially of the more exotic kind.

Sonnet 28

Qu'écrirez-vous sur ces tablettes?: 'What will you write upon these pages?'
toute à vous: 'All yours'.

Sonnet 30

Tolstoy: Count F.P. Tolstoy (1783–1873), a well known and fashionable artist.

Sonnet 31

Yazikov, N.M.: (1803–46), an acquaintance of Pushkin and minor poet.

Sonnet 32

the dagger, mask and trumpet: symbols of (out-of-date) classical drama. *odes*: To Pushkin odes represented the pretentious and ponderous style of 18th-century poetry, to which Pushkin preferred romantic and shorter elegiac lyric poetry.

Sonnet 33

As Others See It: Reference to a satire by I. Dmitriev (1760–1837) concerning the relative merits of odes and romantic elegies.

Sonnet 37

Byronic, he'd then swim across/ this Hellespont: The original contains a (now relatively obscure) reference to Byron's *The Corsair*. Byron himself swam the Hellespont, which Pushkin knew from *Don Juan* (II,cv).

Sonnet 43

de Pradt, Dominique: (1759–1837) French political writer.

Sonnet 45

Hippocrene: A spring on Mount Helicon, in Greek mythology sacred to the muses.

Sonnet 47

between the hours of wolf and dog: Time of the day when it is too dark for a shepherd to distinguish between the two animals.

Sonnet 50

Lafontaine: August (1758–1851), German author of novels on family life.

Notes on Chapter 5

Sonnet 2

Kibitka: A type of Russian hooded sledge.

Sonnet 3

Another poet: The reference is to the poem 'First Snow' by Prince Vyazemski (Pushkin's note). The Prince (1792–1878) was a friend of the poet.
. . . that bard who lauds his Finnish maid: The reference is to the descriptions of the Finnish winter in Baratïnski's 'Eda' (Pushkin's note).

Sonnet 8

. . . the wax within the dish: hot wax was poured into cold water, whereupon it assumed 'prophetic shapes'.
the time-honoured ditty: "The peasants . . . ": A folk song portending death for the elderly.
. . . the charming little cat: Folk song foretelling marriage.

Sonnet 9

Agafon!: The name comes as a grotesque shock. Nabokov writes in his commentary: 'We should imagine an English young lady of 1820 slipping out of the manor gate to ask a passing labourer his name and

discovering that her husband will be called not Allan but Noah.'
The whole of this passage describes various tricks young girls got up
to in order to find out their future husband's name.

Sonnet 10

Svetlana: Another reference to Zhukovski's ballad of that name (see
Chapter 3, sonnet 5). Here Svetlana is also practising divination in
the fashion just described.

Sonnet 22

Martin Zadeck: According to Nabokov probably an invented name
for a German-Swiss soothsayer who died around 1770. The work
attributed to him seems to have first appeared in Moscow in 1814,
remaining popular well into the 19th century.

Sonnet 23

Malvina: by Mme Cottin, who also wrote 'Mathilde' (see Chapter 4,
sonnet 8).
Marmontel: (1723–99) French author.

Sonnet 26

Buyánov: Character in a racy verse narrative by Pushkin's uncle Vasiliy
Pushkin (1770–1830). The fluff is characteristic of the squalid drunk
of Russian humour, who slept on a dirty floor or a decrepit feather
bed.

Sonnet 32

Tsimlyanski: a sparkling wine.
Zizí: one of Pushkin's mistresses. According to Nabokov, she was a
little on the plump side, so the comparison is intended as a joke.

Sonnet 35

ombre, Boston: ombre is a card game of Spanish origin, and both are games related to whist.

Sonnet 40

Francesco Albani: (aka Albano) 1578–1660, once immensely popular Italian painter, now almost entirely forgotten.

Sonnet 44

cotillon: simple French dance of the age of Louis XIV. An anglicised version of the name, 'cotillion', apparently exists. However, more than fifty years of close association with music has kept this from me until now. A French cotillon it has always been, and so it shall remain in this translation.

Notes on Chapter 6

Motto

'There, where the days are misty and short, a race is born that does not fear death'.

Sonnet 4

five versts: Just over three miles, or five and a half kilometres.

Sonnet 5

Regulus: Roman general (c. 250 B.C.) of the 1st Punic War, sent home by the Carthaginians with a harsh offer of peace. Having given his captors his word that he would go back, he nevertheless encouraged the Romans to continue the war, knowing that on his return he would be put to death. Hence the word 'renewed' in line 13, referring to Zaretski and *his* fate, in contrast to that of Regulus.

Sonnet 7

Sed alia tempora!: Latin for, as Bob Dylan has it, 'The times, they are a changin''.

Sonnet 20

Delvig: Baron Anton Delvig (1798–1831) a minor poet and one of Pushkin's closest friends.

Notes on Chapter 7

Sonnet 4

Lyóvshin: (1746–1826) minor author of novels and tragedies, as well as works on horticulture.
Priam: Last king of Troy, a gentle old man.

Sonnet 14

brother: Conventional Russian term of endearment for a close personal friend of one's own age.

Sonnet 19

The reference in the last two lines is, of course, to Napoleon.

Sonnet 22

Don Juan: Byron's narrative poem (1818–25) *The Giaour*, poem by Byron, 1813.

Sonnet 24

Harold: (Byron's *Childe Harold's Pilgrimage*) Regarding the deeper references in sonnets 22–24, the reader is most warmly advised (as in all other aspects of EO) to study the relevant pages in Nabokov's voluminous and glorious commentary to Pushkin's masterpiece.

Sonnet 32

as in a house . . . the windows whitened with chalk: The reference is to a deserted house, the windows of which have been whitened as part of closing it down. It is, with the rest of the passage, a most effective metaphor for the dead and now pale Lenski.

Sonnet 37

Petrovsky Castle: Built in 1776, burnt by the French in 1812, but rebuilt in 1840.

Sonnet 38

Bokharans: Inhabitants of a Russian province north of Afghanistan, who sold oriental goods, such as Samarkand carpets and robes.

Sonnet 40

St. Chariton's: Church in East Moscow, in which area Pushkin spent several happy childhood years.

Sonnet 41

'Pachette' See note on sonnet 33, chapter 2.
St. Simeon's: Church dedicated to the Syrian hermit St. Simeon Stylites, who spent thirty-seven years upon a pillar.

Sonnet 49

Vyazemski: Friend of Pushkin, and the same poet whose poem '*First Snow*' is referred to in sonnet 3, chapter 5, and from whom the motto to chapter one is taken.

Sonnet 50

Melpómené's: The muse of tragedy.
Thalia: the comic muse.

Sonnet 51

Sobránie: Moscow meeting place of the Russian aristocracy.

Notes on Chapter 8

Sonnet 1

Lyceum: School established outside St. Petersburg at Tsarskoe Selo for young aristocrats in 1810, and opened with Pushkin among its first pupils on October 19th, 1811. This date was celebrated in various poems by Pushkin throughout his life, and the friends he made there between 1811 and 1817 remained close to him.
Apuleius: Second century Roman writer, best know today as the author of the salacious tale, *The Golden Ass*, in contrast to the masterly (and thus, by implication, boring) Latin prose of Cicero.

Sonnet 2

Derzhávin, G.R. (1743–1816): Most renowned Russian poet of the 18th century. Pushkin, aged 16, recited a poem to him at the Lyceum, and was duly praised.

Sonnet 4

Leonore: Heroine of Gottfried Bürger's (1747–94) famous romantic eponymous ballad.
Tauris: Old name for the Crimea.
Nereids: Sea nymphs, and daughters to the sea-god Nereus.

Sonnet 5

Moldavia: Province of Bessarabia, in extreme SW Russia.
steppes: reference to one of Pushkin's poems, *The Gypsies* (1823–24).

Sonnet 12

Demon: Reference to Pushkin's poem *The Demon* (1823).

Sonnet 13

Chatski: The hero of a comedy by Griboedov, *Woe from Wit* (1824). After three years abroad he turns up in Moscow on the very day the girl he loves is having a party.

Sonnet 14

What's that in Russian? I don't know!: A jibe at Admiral Alexander Shishkov (1754–1841), statesman, writer and vehement opponent of Gallicisms and liberal thought in general. The name was omitted from the first editions of EO, but hinted at in the fair copy.

Sonnet 16

Nina Voronskýa: The name is a stylised generalisation, representing the 'typical' Russian society beauty of the day, although real-life names have been suggested as a model, 'a dreary and fundamentally inept question', according to Nabakov.

Sonnet 25

bemedalled sisters: Two ladies-in-waiting of the empress, on whom a royal insignia had been bestowed.

Sonnet 26

Prolázov: The name means something like 'sycophant', and was often used for figures of ridicule in 18th century Russian comedies.
Saint-Priest: According to Nabakov, the reference is to Count Emmanuil Sen-Pri (1806–28), reported to have been an accomplished caricaturist.

Sonnet 35

Gibbon . . . Bayle:
E. Gibbon (1737–94): The English historian.
J.J. Rousseau (1712–78): The French writer.

J.G. Herder (1744–1803): German philosopher.

S. Chamfort (1740–94): French writer of epigrams and maxims.

A. Manzoni (1785–1873): Italian romantic novelist and poet.

Madame de Staël (1766–1817): The French writer whose novel *Delphine* was among Tatiana's favourites (see note on Chapter 3, sonnet 10).

M. F. X. Bichat (1771–1802): French anatomist, physician, and writer.

S. A. Tissot (1728–1797): Swiss doctor and writer.

B. Fontenelle 1657–1757): French philosopher of the Enlightenment.

P. Bayle (1647–1706): French sceptic and philosopher, precursor of the Enlightenment.

e sempre bene 'That's all right, then.'

Sonnet 38

magnetism: Old name for hypnotism. Here an ironic reference to a fashion of the time.

'Benedetta', *'Idol mio'*: the opening words of two Italian songs popular at the time.

Sonnet 51

Sadi: Famous 13th century Persian poet.

'A few are absent, some departed.': Generally taken as an oblique reference to the executed or exiled participants of the failed 'Decembrist' revolt of December 1825.

Dedalus European Classics

Dedalus European Classics began in 1984 with D.H. Lawrence's translation of Verga's *Mastro Don Gesualdo*. In addition to rescuing major works of literature from being out of print, the editors' other major aim was to redefine what constituted a 'classic'.

Titles available include:

Little Angel – Andreyev   £4.95
The Red Laugh – Andreyev   £4.95
Séraphita (and other tales) – Balzac   £6.99
The Quest of the Absolute – Balzac   £6.99
The Episodes of Vathek – Beckford   £6.99
The Devil in Love – Cazotte   £5.99
Misericordia – Galdos   £8.99
Spirite – Gautier   £6.99
The Dark Domain – Grabinski   £6.99
The Life of Courage – Grimmelshausen   £6.99
Simplicissimus – Grimmelshausen   £10.99
Tearaway – Grimmelshausen   £6.99
The Cathedral – Huysmans   £7.99
En Route – Huysmans   £7.99
The Oblate – Huysmans   £7.99
Parisian Sketches – Huysmans   £6.99
The Other Side – Kubin   £9.99
The Mystery of the Yellow Room – Leroux   £8.99
The Perfume of the Lady in Black – Leroux   £8.99
The Woman and the Puppet – Louÿs   £6.99
Blanquerna – Lull   £7.95
The Angel of the West Window – Meyrink   £9.99
The Golem – Meyrink   £6.99
The Green Face – Meyrink   £7.99
The Opal (and other stories) – Meyrink   £7.99
The White Dominican – Meyrink   £6.99

Walpurgisnacht – Meyrink   £6.99
Ideal Commonwealths – More/Bacon et al   £7.95
Smarra & Trilby – Nodier   £6.99
The Late Mattia Pascal – Pirandello   £7.99
The Notebooks of Serafino Gubbio – Pirandello   £7.99
Tales from the Saragossa Manuscript – Potocki   £5.99
Manon Lescaut – Prévost   £7.99
Cousin Bazilio – Queiroz   £11.99
The Crime of Father Amaro – Queiroz   £11.99
The Mandarin – Queiroz   £6.99
The Relic – Queiroz   £9.99
The Tragedy of the Street of Flowers – Querioz   £9.99
Baron Munchausen – Raspe   £6.99
Bruges-la-Morte – Rodenbach   £6.99
The Maimed – Ungar   £6.99
The Class – Ungar   £7.99
I Malavoglia (The House by the Medlar Tree) –
   Verga   £7.99
Mastro Don Gesualdo – Verga   £7.99
Short Sicilian Novels – Verga   £ 6.99
Sparrow, Temptation & Cavalleria Rusticana –
   Verga   £8.99
Micromegas – Voltaire   £4.95

Manon Lescaut – Abbé Prévost

'The tragic love story *Manon Lescaut* has been the model for operas (by Puccini, Massenet and Henze) and films for years. This French classic by Abbé Prévost, retranslated for the first time in 52 years by Steve Larkin, shows remarkable resiliency more than 200 years after its original publication. Set in Paris and Louisiana around 1720, it is the archetypal 18th-century romance, with the noble des Grieux as devoted lover and the worldly Manon as inconstant mistress.'
  Publisher's Weekly

'Manon is the perfidious object of the Chevalier des Grieux's affections. She betrays him; his love for her threatens his every moral tenet, yet he clings to a belief in the redemptive power of love. *Manon Lescaut* is both operatic high tragedy and picaresque adventure. As Larkin's introduction emphasises, the ambiguity of the Jesuitical Des Grieux means that this love is far from innocent, and an enduring puzzle.'
  Isobel Montgomery in *The Guardian*

£7.99   ISBN 1 873982 77 1   182p   B.Format

Simplicissimus – Grimmelshausen

'*Simplicissimus* is the eternal innocent, the simple-minded survivor, and we follow him from a childhood in which he loses his parents to the casual atrocities of occupying troops, through his own soldiering adventures, and up to his final vocation as a hermit alone on an island. It is Rabelasian in some respects, but more down to earth and melancholy.'
 Phil Baker in *The Sunday Times*

'It is the rarest kind of monument to life and literature, for it has survived almost three centuries and will survive many more. It is a story of the most basic kind of grandeur – gaudy, wild, raw, amusing, rollicking and ragged, boiling with life, on intimate terms with death and evil – but in the end, contrite and fully tired of a world wasting itself in blood, pillage and lust, but immortal in the miserable splendour of its sins.'
 Thomas Mann

£10.99   ISBN 1 873982 78 X   434p   B.Format

Life of Courage – Grimmelshausen

'Courage – the name is her euphemism for the only manlike aggressive tool she lacks – can outfight, outwit and outf—k any man, and she is beautiful. In English, her progency includes Defoe's *Moll Flanders* and *Roxana*, Cleland's *Fanny Hill*, and Southern and Hoffenberg's *Candy*, in German, Brecht took her name and period for *Mother Courage*. In Mitchell's snappy translation, the first since 1912, she is one helluva woman.'

Ray Olson in *Booklist*

'A companion volume to Mitchell's (equally fine) earlier translation of Grimmelshausen's classic 1688 satire *Simplicissimus*, this defiant earthy first-person narrative (which followed it closely, in 1670) contains the "confession" of the resourceful camp follower and entrepreneur who schemed and prospered throughout the carnage of the Thirty Years' War (1618–48) and inspired the eponymous heroine of Brecht's epic political play *Mother Courage and Her Children* in Grimmelshausen's hands, Courage is a resolutely apolitical survivor: a highborn beauty brought low, who combats social and sexual disenfranchisement and victimization with a gusto that blithely negates her creator's intermittent moralizing, and puts her in a class with Defoe's *Moll Flanders*. A rich, sly entertainment.'

Kirkus Reviews

£6.99   ISBN 1 873982 18 4   175p   B.Format

Tearaway – Grimmelshausen

'*Tearaway* first published in 1670, is the third Johann Grimmelshausen novel to feature Simplicius and tells of the further encounters and exploits of this rather brazen traveller, with the horrors of the Thirty Years War looming in the background. Written in a direct narrative, the prose is just as engaging 333 years on.'

Ian Maxen in *What's On in London*

'Johann Grimmelshausen was born in early 17th-century Germany and fought in the Thirty Years War before becoming a writer, flavouring his memoirs with a sense of the fantastical story and fascinating yarn. *Tearaway* is the sequel to the German classic *Simplicissimus* which recounted the life of the author in the war and his many escapades across Europe involving his wife, fellow soldiers and any number of unlikely characters from the west coast of France to the eastern borders of Turkey. Eventually destined to live his remaining days as a one legged fiddler begging, stealing and cheating his way across his homeland he certainly lived a life getting there, however unlikely may be some of the tales he tells.'

Buzz Magazine

£6.99   ISBN 1 903517 18 4   167p   B.Format

I Malavoglia – Giovanni Verga

'This is a tragic tale of poverty, honour and survival in a society where the weak go to the wall unmourned.'
    The Sunday Times

I Malavoglia is one of the great landmarks of Italian Literature. It is so rich in character, emotion and texture that it lives forever in the imagination of all who read it. What Verga called in his preface a ';sincere and dispassionate study of society' is an epic struggle against poverty and the elements by the fishermen of Aci Trezza, told in an expressive language based on their own dialect.

'Giovanni Verga's novel of 1881 *I Malavoglia* presented its translator Judith Landry with formidable problems of dialect and peasant speech which she has solved so unobtrusively that one wonders why this moving and tragic tale is so little known in England.'
    Margaret Drabble in *The Observer's Books of the Year*

'This is a tragic tale of poverty, honour and survival in a society where the weak go to the wall unmourned.'
    The Sunday Times

'*I Malavoglia* obsessed me from the moment I read it. And when the chance came I made a film of it, *La Terra Trema*.'
    Luchino Visconti

£7.99   1 873982 13 5   268p   B.Format

The Crime of Father Amaro – Eça de Queiroz

'A major source of pleasure and one of its many strengths is its wide-ranging panoply of perspectives, its generosity in assigning chapters to be fleshed out by the lesser characters and its depiction of their idiosyncracies: the pious and easily offended pharmacist Carlos; the gluttonous Libaninho with his penchant for rice puddings and port; and the lazy, sleezy Canon Dias, Amaro's superior, who becomes a gloating accessory to his crimes.'

Daniel Lukes in *The Times Literary Supplement*

'*The Crime of Father Amaro* is also the best possible introduction to Portuguese literature. It is the first great realistic novel in the language; a product of the wonderful period when it seemed to be easy, all over Europe, to write novels of the highest literary quality which were also commercial successes. So it is instantly approachable, while at the same time complex and ultimately mysterious. All these riches are made available in a brand new translation. When *The Crime of Father Amaro* was first translated, very inadequately, in the sixties, it still made quite a stir, but was quickly forgotten. Dedalus deserve every credit for promoting Eça once again. Margaret Jull Costa's new translation is far better than the earlier one. She translates everything, for one thing (the sixties version is full of omissions). She shows considerable skill and tact in handling the tricky problems posed by Portuguese names, of people and of places, and by the technical vocabulary of the Church. These things, the curse of poor translators, are treated simply and naturally without the need for footnotes. The rich patterning of the text survives as a deeply satisfying experience.'

Tom Earle in *The London Magazine*

'a work of mesmerizing literary power.'

Michael Dirda in *The Washington Post*

£11.99   ISBN 1 873982 89 5   471p   B.Format

Cousin Bazilio – Eça de Queiroz

'Sauciness and scandal come as part of the enticing package in this 1878 European classic by Portugal's most celebrated 19th-century writer. *Cousin Bazilio* might not be his best work, but it certainly drew the most attention when it was originally published, for all the wrong reasons; specifically deceitful lusts, a series of characters – some aristocratic hedonistic socialites, others colourful aspiring servants, but all connected by a string of naughty secrets. The tale rips along at a pace that could outdo any modern soap, while the social realist side of de Queiroz shows up the hypocritical limitations laid down by society, particularly on female morality. A classic then, but distinctly alternative in every way.'
The Scotsman

'Adultery, blackmail, sentimentality and lust all come under Eça's scrutiny. Sins are scattered amid a gallery of vivid characters, central of which are the adulterous heroine, her first love, the cuckolded husband, and most importantly, the maid. This cunning portrayal of life below stairs casts a cold eye across the hypocrisy of "respectability," recreating the sultry summer heat of Lisbon and the tensions and passions underlying both the refinements of the wealthy and the loyalty of the servants. Sheer brilliance.'
The Good Book Guide

£11.99   ISBN 1 903517 08 7   439p   B.Format

The Tragedy of the Street of Flowers – Eça de Queiroz

"An unexpected bonus: the belated English publication of a work by Portugal's great but little-known novelist, Eça de Queiroz, who died 100 years ago and bears comparison with Balzac and Flaubert. *The Tragedy of the Street of Flowers* unrolls a fascinating panorama – colour, animated and satirically observed – of 19th-century Portugal, from its mouldering provincial towns to the flashy falsities of the capital.'
Peter Kemp in *The Sunday Times Books of the Year*

'Attractive and repellent by turns, Genoveva is a splendid creation who almost achieves stature and sympathy sufficient for tragedy in a novel otherwise suffused with irony and bathos. Through her, Eça anatomises Portuguese society, cutting through its superficial elegance to the inadequacy and insecurity he discerns – with sympathy – underneath. *The Tragedy of the Street of Flowers* justifies his claim to be numbered among the great European novelists of his day.'
Paul Duguid in *The Times Literary Supplement*

'The pressing logic of the plot, the clarity and occasional lyricism of the prose, as well as the mastery of dialogue, make Queiroz a formidable author, so it is more surprising that translations of his books in English are so rare. Huge praise, then, to the publishers for their determination to make available major works that are otherwise neglected in Anglophone countries, and to the translator, Margaret Jull Costa, whose achievement is giving the impression that Queiroz might have written the English himself.'
Henry Sheen in *The New Statesman*

£9.99   ISBN 1 873982 64 X   346p   B.Format

ML

40/9